M000074713

TALES OF
MUNDANE MAGIC
Volume One

Shaina Krevat

TALES OF MUNDANE MAGIC

A Shaina Krevat book

Copyright © 2018 by Shaina Krevat
All rights reserved.

ISBN: 978-1-7325013-0-0

P.O. Box 5901, Santa Monica, CA 90409

talesofmundanemagic.com

Cover illustration by Gloria Kang.

PRINTED IN THE UNITED STATES OF AMERICA

To my loving parents,
who have always supported my creativity

Table of Contents

Gertie and Bridget build a snowman

As snowflakes danced down from thick clouds, Ziggy the ghost dog had fun trying to catch them on his tongue. Since his mouth was incorporeal, the challenge was dead on arrival, but that didn't hinder his joy.

Bridget Mallon, one of Ziggy's owners during his life, was bundled up against the chill. She was thrilled about the first snow of the season. With first semester finals fast approaching at Flories Boarding School, it was nice to take an afternoon off from studying.

While Bridget admired how pretty the school looked draped in snow and ice, her older sister Gertie, wrapped in layers and topped with a black magician's hat, packed together a snowball in her hands.

Bridget turned to see how her sister was faring.

"Well?" she asked.

"It's good," Gertie said, tossing the snowball back and

forth between her hands. "Not too wet, not too dry-"

She missed the ball, and it fell to the ground.

Ziggy, barking in delight, flew under the snowball to try to catch it. His attempt was, again, in vain, but he shook out his wispy fur, looked up at Gertie with his tongue hanging out, and waited with a wagging tail for the next throw.

Gertie, unfortunately, couldn't see him at the moment. As Ziggy was a ghost, he was invisible to most living beings. Bridget, on the other hand, could still see him. Her left eye had been ruined in an accident many years ago, but because of this, it was imbued with magic, allowing her to see many things that normal eyes shouldn't. Including ghosts.

Normally, Gertie wore an enchanted baseball cap that allowed her to see Ziggy, but as it didn't allow for much warmth, it was currently stuffed in one of her jacket pockets. Another one of her many hats - this one a beanie - was pulled over her ears, under the top hat that didn't keep out the chill.

"Snowman time!" Bridget said, bouncing on her toes.

Gertie grinned. "Okay, so I have a hat," she tipped the top hat. "You have a nose…"

Bridget held up the large carrot she had been keeping in her pocket.

"Did you bring sticks and rocks?" Gertie asked.

"Uh," Bridget said, looking on the ground beneath them. "I'll go look for arm sticks in the woods."

"I'll find some pebbles," Gertie said. "Meet back here?"

Bridget nodded.

The two sisters went off. Ziggy followed Gertie, hoping for another throw of a snowball.

Bridget wandered into the sprinkling of trees at the edge of Flories Boarding School's property. If she had kept going, and managed to circumvent the magical wall that protected the school, the trees would get taller, and thicker, and evolve into the dark woods, where creatures and magic of old histories still survived.

But not too far into the woods, she found a good sized tree branch on the ground, and then another, so she stopped to pick them up.

She was about to head back to the rendezvous point, but out of the corner of her left eye - the eye that could see things normal eyes couldn't - Bridget saw a shimmer. She turned, and could barely make out an enchanted lump in what looked like a naturally occurring hollow in the snow. Curious, she put down her sticks slowly, not wanting to startle whatever it was, and kneeled low to the ground. When she saw no movement under the enchantment, Bridget started creeping towards what seemed to be an animal lying under an invisibility spell.

But before Bridget could get much closer, a reindog blocked her path, shaking off its conjured camouflage that had made it sparkle like ice.

Bridget had heard of reindogs before, but had never seen

one up close. They were able to conceal themselves to magical levels, blending in seamlessly with their surroundings unless they moved. The reindogs looked like slim canines, with longer legs and snouts and short fluffy tails. Both males and females had horns that curled around their floppy triangular ears, and their fur changed color with the weather. The reindog standing in front of Bridget had fur that was mostly white and grey with some remaining brown patches.

Its eyes seemed soft and begging as it snuffed at Bridget's jacket.

Bridget realized what it must have been smelling. She reached in and pulled the carrot from her pocket.

The reindog took a big bite, making the tip of the carrot poke visibly into its cheek, and went back toward the enchanted spot in the snow. Bridget followed it, and saw that there was a burrow that held another adult reindog curled up around two puppies. The youngsters almost looked like normal dogs if not for the gangliness of their legs and their stubs of tails, and sat up mewling as their parent approached.

Bridget watched with a smile as the reindog spat out the carrot for them to eat. The puppies began fighting over it, nibbling what bites they could. Satisfied with her discovery, Bridget picked up the branches and headed back to the snowman.

"Nice arms," Gertie said with a grin. The two lower balls of snow were done, and she was working on the third.

"You'll never guess what I saw!" Bridget said, her nose red and eyes sparkling.

Gertie held back a laugh at her sister's enthusiasm, hefting up the last snowball to place for the snowman's head. "Flying fish?" she joked.

Bridget laughed. "No-."

"Hold on," Gertie said, plopping the snowball on the snowman's body. She placed the small stones she had found as eyes, mouth, and buttons and Bridget stuck the stick arms in place.

"Nose?" Gertie asked. Bridget pulled out the stump of the carrot that the reindog had left.

"What happened to it?" Gertie asked.

Bridget seemed ready burst. "I fed it to a reindog!"

Gertie's eyes opened wide in wonder. "Lucky!" she said. "Much better than flying fish!"

Bridget stuck the mangled carrot nose into the snowman's face with a triumphant thump.

"All right, now for the best part!" Gertie said, removing the top hat from her head and placing it onto the snowman's.

The snowman's right arm began waving.

"Hi there," it said, though its dotted line of a mouth didn't move. "Happy holidays!"

"I bought it online," Gertie admitted. "I thought it'd be interesting."

"It's cute!" Bridget said, high-fiving the waving arm.

"Snow is fun!" the snowman said.

"Good," Gertie said, clapping the snow off her gloves. "Because the hat is totally worthless for anything else."

"It's a cool addition to your collection," Bridget pointed out.

Gertie pulled out her phone to take a video of the talking snowman.

"Hi there," it declared. "Winter is my favorite time of year!"

Bridget suddenly saw something that wasn't there - a flash of the future. It was a feeling she had become intimately familiar with in the years since her accident. Wind howling, snow swirling, trees falling down. And then it was gone.

The icy air was racking through her lungs, her breathing panicked. Bridget realized she was kneeling in the snow, her legs starting to go numb. Gertie was crouching in front of her, gripping one of Bridget's hands in both of hers.

"What'd you see?" Gertie asked, reaching forward to rub the side of Bridget's arm in comfort.

"Snowstorm," she responded, a glint of terror in her eyes.

Gertie nodded, stood, and immediately pulled the hat off the snowman.

It just managed to get out, "Isn't snow won-?" before freezing in place.

Ziggy barked and Bridget turned. The little family of reindogs had managed to follow her.

"No!" Bridget shouted. She could already see the darkening of the sky. "Go back! You'll be safe in your burrow."

"No time," Gertie said, grabbing the carrot stump from the snowman and holding it out toward the reindogs. She whistled. "Come on! Here little reindogs, you'll be okay!"

Ziggy yipped and tried to herd them towards the girls, but despite their magical prowess, the reindogs couldn't see him.

They could see, and smell, the carrot, however. The little puppies followed Gertie eagerly, floundering through the snow, while their parents followed along slowly, wary of the humans.

The winds were beginning to pick up, sending Bridget's long hair twisting this way and that. The snowman's hat was nearly carried away, but Gertie clung to it while leading the reindogs to safety. One of the puppies fell with a yelp, but its parent picked it up by the scruff of its neck and carried on.

The big door of Bridget's dorm building was held shut by the whistling of the wind, but with a countdown and a pull, the sisters yanked it open.

"Fetch!" Gertie shouted, flinging the carrot into the common room.

Barking in harmony, Ziggy and all four reindogs ran inside the building, and the girls pulled the door shut behind them as the snow started churning through the air with a vengeance.

❀ ❀ ❀

"My roommates are going to love this," Bridget said sarcastically, gesturing to all the muddy footprints and shed fur. She and Gertie pet one adult reindog while the others cuddled by the warm fire in the center of the common area of Bridget's floor. Ziggy, curled up by her side, yawned in agreement.

"We'll wait for the storm to be over and then the reindogs will be back outside," Gertie assured her.

The puppies looked up from the fire to Bridget, their large brown eyes begging.

"Okay, okay," she said. Bridget went to the kitchen, sighing as she pulled a fresh bunch of carrots from the fridge.

Gertie and Bridget go to a funeral

It was a lovely winter day. Snow slush had been pushed to line the sidewalks as more flakes fell on eyelashes and noses alike. Leafless trees were tickled by the wind, streetlamps glowed warmly, and fogs formed from breathy laughter. Gertie watched passersby with interest, at least until the funeral planner closed the curtains. Gertie sighed. Count on her Great Grandma Gertrude (her namesake) to pass from old age on Midwinter's Eve to guarantee the entire family would be together for the holidays.

The room was close to frigid. Gertie eyed the fireplace, sitting under a coat of arms with trumpets, wondering why it wasn't lit. There were tables of food and drink in the back of the large room and Gertie swallowed as her mouth watered. Why hadn't she eaten lunch?

Gertie's gaze continued to scan the room, over her extended family, all shifting about awkwardly while listening to eulogies, same as her. An air of gloom had set over her normally boisterous, magical family, and it was difficult to see them this way. Great Grandma Gertrude wouldn't have wanted this. Gertie finally settled on staring wistfully at an organ, shoved in a corner in the back with dust choking it, used for little more than decoration. If only she knew how to play.

Her father, Theodore Mallon, nudged her with his elbow. "I know it's miserable," he said. "But we'll get through it."

Gertie turned back to the proceedings and nodded. She felt for the paper folded in her pocket, checking it hadn't slipped out. It was a letter from her mother that she was supposed to read at the podium, apologizing for her absence and recalling fond memories of her grandmother. Gertie and her sister wished their mother could be there as well, but work was work, airfare was expensive during the holidays, and with deadlines fast approaching and emergency after emergency popping up, there was nothing her mom could do.

Bridget slumped farther in her seat, trying to brush her hair to cover her magic eye. It did no good. While people spoke at the podium, all the poor girl could focus on was the ghost of Great Grandma Gertrude, scowling over the whole affair.

The spirit looked exactly as she had the last time Bridget had seen her great grandmother (before the funeral, of course). Her gray hair was a fiery mane flickering about her head, her body small and thin, her features soft and wrinkled despite her expression of derision at the display before her.

Bridget was used to seeing ghosts, in the years since the loss of her eye. It wasn't a comfortable feeling, but most spirits ignored her and she did the same. This was different. She had never experienced seeing the ghost of someone she had known in life. Except for Ziggy of course.

But Ziggy was different. He was a dog, not a blood relative.

Grandma Leona was sniffling, lamenting the loss of her mother in her grand dramatic fashion at the podium.

"She was taken from us far too soon." Grandma Leona stopped for a sob.

"Posh," Great Grandma Gertrude muttered, audible to Bridget. "After a hundred and eighteen years I'm ready for peace."

Ziggy, hovering over the seat next to Bridget, barked in agreement.

"Hush," Bridget whispered to the dog's ghost.

He panted a smile up at her and bounded up to lick her from chin to nose. A bone-deep chill ran through Bridget's jaw and she sneezed.

Gertie looked over, raising her eyebrows. Bridget just shook her head. Her older sister didn't need to know the ruckus that happened when ghosts saw their own funerals. They were never pleased.

"Bridget, darling," Great Grandma Gertrude called from across the hall, where she perched on a grandfather clock. "Would you tell your grandmother that this is a time for celebration? That my life was wonderful, and she should honor the spirit of it?"

Bridget covered her face in her hands. Of course her great grandmother would know she could see and hear her. She had helped Bridget explore the secrets of her mansion when Bridget was just a girl, and learn the capabilities of her ruined eye.

"Is Ziggy being that bad?" Gertie whispered. Having to dress formally, Gertie was forbidden (forbidden!) from wearing her baseball cap, which was spelled to let her see their beloved dog.

"Not him," Bridget muttered back.

"Who?"

"Great Grandma Gertrude."

"Oh." Gertie frowned. "Does she not like the service?"

"Stop crying!" Gertrude had moved to hover in front of her son, Great Uncle Maury. "I specifically asked for dancing! Where's my music? Surely they knew I'd be here!"

"She wants this to be a party," Bridget muttered. "She's upset that they didn't listen."

"I remember," Grandma Leona said, still giving her heartfelt eulogy, "when I was a girl, and afraid to go swimming in our pool because someone," she gave a fond look to her brother, "told me that pixie fish lived in the bottom. And mother - she didn't say the reasonable thing, which would have been that pixie fish live in saltwater - she said, 'You can be afraid at what lies at the bottom, or you can jump in and see if you can make friends with it.'" Grandma Leona sniffed. "I think that's advice we can all take to heart."

Great Grandma Gertrude smiled at that.

"I guess, all that's left to say, is goodbye, mother." Grandma Leona looked back to large picture of the Mallons' matriarch, placed next to her casket.

Gertrude sighed, and floated over to the empty seat next to Bridget, who stiffened.

"They didn't even choose a flattering picture," the ghost said.

Bridget finally looked over and made eye contact with her great grandma. "They expected you to move on," she whispered. "What unfinished business could you have? You lived over a century! Whatever you needed to do you had the time to finish."

Great Grandma Gertrude grinned. "That's my girl." She brushed Bridget's hair back from her eye. The cold pierced through Bridget again and she sneezed.

"Blow your nose," her father said.

Bridget sniffed. "I'm fine."

There was silence as Great Uncle Maury shuffled up to talk. He cleared his throat. "I'm not as good at speaking as my sister." Instead, he pulled a large mirror out of his expandable bag. "I thought I'd just...show some of my favorite memories of my mother."

What flickered across the mirror at a wave of his hand was a montage of his mother's laugh, of her baking in the kitchen for him, of toys and magic and jokes. Of parties in Gertrude's mansion, surrounded by friends and family.

"That's what I'm looking for," Gertrude said, floating towards the ceiling and pointing at the memories. "One last time."

Bridget looked away from the ghost and saw her sister raising her eyebrows in concern. "She just wants everyone to have fun," Bridget said.

Gertie's mouth thinned as the congregation politely applauded Great Uncle Maury's heartfelt display. Sweeping her choice of formal hat onto her head - a black, wide-brimmed number with a fluffy purple feather that Great Grandma Gertrude herself had given her - Gertie cut off her aunt and took to the podium. "Friends, family. I too am going to miss Great Grandma Gertrude. I share her name, and for years, you all have said that I share her spirit. And in that spirit," Gertie said with a twinkle in her eye, "I think we should celebrate the wonderful life that the Mallon matriarch had."

Gertie waved her hand, and with the powers granted to her by her hat, the decorative trumpets above the fireplace began to sing. Bridget sighed under a wave of relief. Her great grandmother's ghost was grinning.

"Great Grandma Gertrude loved music," Gertie continued. The wooden tables - those for setting drinks down, not currently bearing food - began to thump rhythmically in time with the horns. "She loved dancing." The decorative organ coughed, and blared in key. "And more than anything, she loved to see her family happy."

Instruments burst in from other rooms, playing along to the upbeat melody that Gertie had cast.

"So let's dance!" Gertie shouted, pulling up family members left and right. Attendees threw the windows open, letting in the light and breeze, and other witches cast their magical spells to add to the music, create colorful lights, and keep out the chill.

Gertie found her way through the crowd, bumping into Bridget halfway.

"Does she like it?" Gertie asked.

Bridget looked to the ghost floating between them, with a beaming smile and tears in her eyes. "She loves it."

Gertie and Bridget deal with a pest

Gertie had a figgle in her bedroom.

The lack of hair clogging her vacuum should have been a sign, as well as the absence of the need to clean off her brush. But she hadn't noticed. Granted, schoolwork was hard, she had been spending time in the gardens gathering potion ingredients, and she'd been away for a weekend to visit her family, but she *should* have noticed.

A figgle was a small creature, limber as a rat with the soul of a cat and the size of a swollen sock. And one of the most annoying pests to get rid of. Humanely, at least.

Figgles were magical, and couldn't be seen with the naked eye, not even an eye like Bridget's. The only way to spy a figgle was in a mirror. They had sensitive eyes and came out of hiding when the light was dim. If a room was empty they might creep out at dusk to eat, but usually they waited until their home's occupant was safely asleep at dawn.

And then they would eat their hair.

Gertie wore a beanie pulled down over her ears, where it would stay until the end of the winter and the bald spot behind her ear grew in. She was staring into the one floor length mirror in her room, trying to see any corners where the little pest might be hiding, when Bridget opened the door with her copy of Gertie's room key.

"I brought the mirrors- ugh." Bridget shivered and dumped an armful of mirrors of various sizes that she had borrowed from her roommates and dorm-mates alike onto Gertie's bed. She pulled the comically-large sweater that she liked to wear from where it was tied at her waist and slipped it over her head. "Why is the outside in here?"

"Oh, my beanie." Gertie rubbed the wool against her head, pushing it up her forehead. "It's charmed for warmth."

"So you're too hot."

"Yep."

"Anyway." Bridget motioned to the pile of mirrors. "Should we set them up?"

The sisters placed the mirrors strategically, so that no matter where the figgle ran in the room they'd be able to see its reflection. Make-up compacts with mirrors were set on desks and the bureau, handheld mirrors were taped on walls and the bed posts, and mirrors that had been stuck in the showers for face-shaving were re-stuck under the desk and on empty spaces on the wall.

It was while the sisters were putting the only other large mirror they had - the one provided by the school for Bridget's room - under the bed on its side that they found where the figgle had been hiding.

It screeched as Gertie brushed against it with her hand and dashed out into the room.

They couldn't see it directly, but its reflection shone true in the mirrors. It sat in the middle of the carpet, sitting up on its thin back paws, its gray feathers in a ruffle and its large pointed nose snuffing in the air.

"Bridget. The cage," Gertie whispered through gritted teeth.

Bridget moved to where she had placed the small rat cage with an art mirror taped to one of the sides and picked it up.

The noise was enough to startle the figgle and it dashed out of view of the mirrors.

It was hard to track its movement across the room, but the girls saw it in one of the compact mirrors when it stopped on top of Gertie's bureau, sniffing the hairbrush Gertie had left out as bait.

Bridget swung the cage toward it, bringing her hand from the opposite direction to try to push it inside.

The figgle struggled against her hand and jumped, curling on her arm with a hiss and batting wildly at her wrist with its claws. Bridget yelled and dropped the cage and Gertie pushed the beastie off her sister's arm and back onto the ground.

It squealed in surprise and dashed back under the bed.

"This is why people buy traps!" Bridget shouted, her free hand covering her bleeding forearm.

"Do you *want* to kill it?" Gertie shouted back, going to her closet for some bandages.

"No!" Bridget accepted the bandages with a grumble. "No, it doesn't deserve that."

"We can do this." Gertie crouched and looked at the figgle's reflection under the bed.

It wiggled its butt, scooting farther back into the corner so only its snout was reflected.

"We can do this," Gertie repeated, sounding less sure this time.

Bridget sighed, kneeling beside her sister, her right forearm bandaged. The bleeding had already stopped. The bandages had a potion on them that would heal minor cuts up in a manner of minutes.

"Have any more hair to spare?" Bridget asked.

"Do you?"

"I can help," a timid voice said from the door.

The girls turned. It was Ernest Yilnog.

The Yilnogs were some of the most powerful witches in the world. They were police, high ranking military members, healers, scientists and the like. They all went to private schools, specifically for witches, not to public boarding schools that happened to feature magical elective tracks like Flories Boarding School. But Ernest did.

Ernest was different than his family. Despite his power - and he was *certainly* the most powerful boy in school - he couldn't use it for healing, or fighting, or inventing new spells, or discovering secrets of the world. No, he could only use it for music.

Sure, it meant that he held concerts in the student gamerooms sometimes, which was the only time people seemed to pay attention to him. It meant he could make things move with a strum of his guitar or with a snap of his fingers. It meant him cleaning his room was a lilt on a flute and he was done. But he wasn't good for much else.

Except, of course, talking about his family. And their accomplishments. And how much about magic and spells he'd known from a young age, despite not being able to practice most of it. About how he didn't need a partner for projects. About how "the actual definition of *seeing* is seeing the future in your mind's eye, not through a magic eye", or how "enchanting should be done using power that comes from the enchanter, not sources like the sun or moon or heat of the earth."

Ernest had managed to piss off almost everyone in the school, but he didn't seem to mind at all. And he certainly never offered to help.

"How can you help?" Gertie demanded.

Ernest didn't answer, instead he started to whistle.

The sisters watched the mirror under the bed as the figgle crept out with its ears pointed forward.

Ernest kept whistling, snapping in rhythm with the music. The figgle stopped in the center of the rug in Gertie's room, sitting on its hind legs and stretching upward, sniffing at Ernest, still standing at the door. Bridget grabbed the cage again and edged slightly closer to the creature. It didn't even notice her.

Bridget put the cage behind the figgle and picked up a nearby shoe with her free hand.

As Ernest's whistles came to a high, pointed trill, Bridget used the sneaker to push the figgle back into the cage. She slammed the door shut, despite its whines.

Bridget lifted the cage to look in the mirror inside. The creature had pressed itself against the woven wire of the cage, staring up at Ernest with wide, begging eyes. It missed the music.

"What do we do with it?" Bridget asked.

"I'll take it," Ernest said, holding his hand out for the cage. "I have all manner of creatures in my room. Frogs and birds and rats and tarantulas-"

Gertie shivered at that one as Bridget handed over the cage.

Ernest looked inside, studying the small figgle, and continued. "They mostly stay there for my music, or if they leave they come back at night. Which is good, because it means they're not bothering anyone else."

He smiled, and it was such a sweet little smile that the girls instantly felt ashamed for the way they excluded him.

"Ernest," Gertie said, "Can I thank you for your help? Do you want to get dinner with us?"

Ernest's face lit up and he nodded. "Let me put him away, and I'll be back with my jacket and wallet."

"Cool."

Ernest took the figgle to his room, and set the cage down on his dresser. The figgle took stock of its new environment, its nose wiggling. Something smelled delicious.

Squeezing against the bars of its cage, the figgle reached out and grabbed Ernest's comb. It chewed on the hair happily. This would do just fine.

Gertie and Bridget go to the library

Gertie stepped into Flories' school library and took a deep breath. The smell of exposed wood, binding glue, and dust greeted her.

The school library had started as the personal collection of Julia Flories, a witch and part-time botanist, whose goal was to create a school that united magic practitioners and non-magically-inclined individuals alike. After her death, it continued to be grown by those who wanted to study her collection and shared her vision to enable others to learn about both the sciences and magic. It was the tallest and deepest building on campus, as far as anyone knew. It stretched so far into the sky that magical bindings were in place in lieu of structurally sound architecture.

"Can I help you?" The woman at the front desk was pleasantly plump, with cheeks that touched the rim of her large glasses as she smiled.

"Yes, thank you," Gertie said. Everyone needed help in this library. It was far too large to just walk around and find what one was looking for. "I'm looking for the Flowers of Dark Meadow series?"

The librarian frowned. "I believe you could check out the electronic version on our website-"

"I like physical books." Gertie shrugged. "I can be old fashioned about some things."

The librarian grinned. "Our young adult selection is on the sixth floor." She pushed a section of her desk and it moved away, granting her an exit, and moved back into place once she was clear. "If you'll follow me…"

The librarian led Gertie to a small wooden platform next to one of the towering bookshelves. The platform was just a step above the normal floor, but it had a wooden waist-high railing nonetheless that the librarian and Gertie ducked under.

Checking to make sure Gertie was next to her, the librarian gripped the railing. "Sixth floor," she said.

The platform shot into the air.

Gertie jolted a bit, not expecting the speed.

The platform lifted through a perfectly sized hole in the second floor, and then the third. Gertie looked down and saw a few teachers on one of the levels, staggering under armfuls of books to distribute to their students.

The platform finally stopped, and Gertie and the librarian

ducked under the railing and paced along the shelves.

"Hm…" The librarian stopped in front of a shelf that was labeled "twelfth century biological sciences". She looked confused.

"What is it?" Gertie asked.

"The young adult fiction should be here."

Gertie squinted, and made out a paper note on one of the higher shelves, next to the sign that labeled the section. "Miss?" She pointed it out to the librarian.

The librarian touched the side of the bookcase.

"Eleventh shelf," she said. The shelves slid out into a staircase, leaving their books to float in their absence. The librarian climbed, and fetched the note.

"Of course." The librarian sighed, stepped back down to Gertie. "It seems one of our ghost librarians moved the young adult fiction section."

"What?"

"They haven't been open to learning the computer system and-" A book flew at the librarian's head and she ducked. She pushed her glasses back up her nose, and Gertie noticed a spark of enchantment on the glass.

"Viola, please." The librarian directed her words to an empty space in the air. "Where did it get moved?"

Gertie watched the librarian tilt her head and listen to the ghost of a former librarian.

"Did you really think that appropriate?" the librarian

asked. She must have heard an answer in the affirmative, because she sighed again.

"One of the librarians moved the young adult section down to the negative tenth level. I can take you-"

The bell at the front desk rang and a ruckus of childish babble floated up. The librarian leaned over the railing and looked down to the ground floor. She bit her lip. "There's a field trip today, I forgot. Give me one moment."

The librarian went to a door labeled "Faculty Only" and returned with a candle. "This will lead you to the right section and shelf." The librarian lit the candle with a match from her pocket. The candle wick sparked with flame for a moment, and a ball of light lifted from the candle all together.

It hung in midair, and the librarian cupped it into her hand. She spoke to it as if it was a person. "Negative tenth floor, section 31W, shelf 12-11. Got that?"

The ball of light danced about in confirmation, and flew through the air back to the platform.

It waited patiently for Gertie to join it.

Gertie stood next to it awkwardly. It didn't move. Gertie placed her hand on the railing, like the librarian had done.

"Negative tenth floor," she said, hesitantly. The platform started plummeting, the candle glow by her side.

Once Gertie and the hovering flame were past the ground floor, there were torches lighting the darkness. Even more comforting, though, was the light that Gertie's little pathfinder granted her.

The platform slowed and stopped, and Gertie ducked under the railing again to stand on the negative tenth floor. As soon as she was gone, the platform flew up and away. Someone else must have called it.

Carefully, in case the platform came back, Gertie stared down the hole for the platform. She saw torch-lined walls as far as the eye could see. It seemed that there was no end to the books in this library.

Gertie turned and took a deep breath. The darkness was intimidating, but at least the familiar scent of books surrounded her.

The maze of bookshelves before her made Gertie stop to consider her choices, but the ball of light zipped forward until it got to an intersection of two aisles. Hesitantly, she followed it. When she caught up, the pathfinder darted to the left and waited at the next turn.

And so it continued. The air started to get warmer, until it was much too hot given Gertie's winter wear.

"How much farther?" Gertie asked, not expecting the pathfinder to answer her. She wondered how the librarians could keep track of the dark halls of books.

Lit torches got fewer and far between, until the only light was the pathfinder.

And then it went out.

It just snuffed out, as if something had purposefully

blown on it, and Gertie was swamped in darkness.

Her eyes started to adjust, and she saw a small figure hiding behind one of the shelves.

"Hello?" Gertie said. She heard a sniffle.

"Can you help me?" The figure asked. It came around the corner until it was a few feet in front of Gertie, and she could see it was a small boy.

"Of course." Gertie kneeled to be at equal height with the boy. "My name's Gertie. What's yours?"

The boy shrugged, averting his gaze shyly.

"Here, come with me," Gertie offered her hand. "We can-"

The boy snatched her hand, his eyes blazing white for a moment, and Gertie screamed.

Bridget fell out of her chair.

"You okay?" Ernest asked.

Ziggy barked, floating above Bridget's head, his stance in full alert.

"No, I mean…" Bridget stood, shaking her head free of the vision. "I'm fine. I think Gertie's in trouble. Or she'll be in trouble soon. I'm not sure."

Ernest looked at his watch.

"I guess you don't want to finish helping me with calculus?"

"Later. Tomorrow." Bridget packed her books up and

started for the door.

"Text if you need my help."

"Will do."

Bridget pulled up the locator app that Gertie had given permission for her to use. It let each sister see the location of the other's phone. The app loaded, showed a spinner for a while and stopped. A text bubble popped up.

We're sorry! It looks like we can't locate Gertie's phone. It might be off or out of range of service right now. Please try again later.

Bridget took a deep breath to calm herself. She slid the phone icon next to Gertie's name to the left and clicked on the emoji of a person.

Warning: Using this app to magically locate the person must only be done in emergencies. If your contact expresses discontent-

Bridget clicked through the alert and waited for the locating spell to do its work.

A dot with Gertie's avatar picture appeared over the school library.

Why wouldn't her phone be working there? Bridget wondered. Ziggy whined and Bridget turned to him.

"Gertie's going to be fine," Bridget told him, and herself as well.

Bridget ran across campus to the library, breaking a sweat from the effort. Ziggy zipped along behind her, tongue and ears flailing in the wind. Bridget would have thought it was adorable if she hadn't been panicking.

They stepped foot inside the library and almost barreled

through a group of kids.

"Woah." Bridget sidestepped a nearby second grader and collapsed on a bench.

A ghost of a mouse screeched from being disturbed and Ziggy barked at it.

"Sh!" a gaunt man in a gray pinstriped suit directed at Ziggy.

Bridget glanced up at him and could only see him with her ruined eye. He was a ghost. If that hadn't clued her in, the fact that he was hovering a foot off the ground did it.

"Sorry," Bridget said. "Where can I find the...living librarian?"

The ghost librarian pointed toward the head of the group of children, who were slowly sitting down at tables at their teacher's direction.

Bridget sighed and waded her way through the class. Ziggy floated behind her.

"Excuse me?"

The librarian turned to Bridget, her hair sticking out of its ponytail and looking quite frazzled.

"If you need help finding a book, you can use one of the computers-"

"No, I..." Bridget sighed. "I think my sister is in trouble in here."

The librarian's brow furrowed in worry. "I knew she was taking too long. She went down to the young adult fiction section, negative tenth floor." She brushed some loose hair behind her ear. "I would go with you, but if I left these kids unsupervised-"

"I understand. Thank you," Bridget said, and ran through the library to the nearest platform.

"No running!" another ghost librarian yelled at her.

She reached a platform, slapped her hands on the railing, and all but shouted, "negative tenth floor."

Ziggy reached Bridget's heels and the platform sped down as if it sensed her urgency.

The platform screeched to a halt and Bridget jumped over the railing.

Ziggy wuffed nervously behind her, and pointed with his nose.

"That way?" Bridget asked.

Ziggy barked again. They headed into the shelves.

As they delved deeper in the library, farther away from the light of the platform's hole, Bridget noticed that many of the torches lining the walls were smoking, as if they had just been extinguished. She warily grabbed the next lit torch she saw.

A few more shelves in and Ziggy got restless. It had been getting warmer and warmer, and Bridget recognized the energy of magic thrumming in the air.

And she could hear something.

Bridget slowed down, whistled for Ziggy to heel, and

held the torch out in front of her warily.

There was a sobbing out in the darkness.

"Hello?" Bridget called.

"Can you help me?" she heard.

A small girl shifted hesitantly into the light.

Or at least it looked like a small girl. Bridget's right eye saw that. But her magic left eye couldn't be deceived. She saw putrid magic, inked words bundled up into a dark chaos that had managed to disguise itself. She saw a tail of energy leading away from the girl like a tether.

"I don't think I can," Bridget said, edging to the right, where the tail led.

"Please?" the girl begged, stepping closer to Bridget.

The dark magic started riling itself up inside the girl. It sparked and threatened at the edges of its girl-shape, almost losing its hold.

"I'm lost myself." Bridget took another step.

The child reached out, and Bridget swung the torch toward her.

The magic inside the girl roared and her voice warped. "Fine then!"

The child's shape twisted and became a black net of magic. It stuck to the shelves, blocking Bridget's escape.

Bridget turned and ran, following the tether.

The creature overturned the shelves, trying to trap Bridget, but as it collapsed on her she dove out of the way.

Ziggy barked, and Bridget looked down to see what the creature was tethered to. A book had fallen onto the ground, pages open and crumpled against the wooden floor.

She lowered the torch she held to its pages and a fire sprung to life.

"No!" The creature shouted, turning red and white as it was devoured. In a matter of moments, it was gone. The book's remains sizzled on the slightly singed wooden floor, ashed pages crumpling into dust.

Bridget took a deep breath.

Ziggy whined and stood on his hind legs, pawing at her hand to get her attention.

"Right," she said. "Let's go."

Bridget ran, following after the speeding dog that would unthinkingly pass through bookshelves that Bridget couldn't.

They came to a door labeled "Faculty Only". Bridget slammed it open, revealing a small room of tables, an ancient computer, and a little boy crouching over Gertie's head on the ground. Bridget looked for where his tether led, and saw the book on Gertie's chest, her hands clutching it as if she needed it there.

"Gertie!" Bridget shouted, and her sister shifted to look at her. Her eyes were so glazed, it was as if she couldn't see anything.

"No!" The boy shouted, and ran to Bridget. He moved faster than Bridget thought possible, and he barrelled her over. The torch in Bridget's hands went flying into the room.

The magic was filthy, the feel of it infecting Bridget's nose. She shoved the boy off of her and heard him hit the wall.

"Bridget?" Gertie murmured.

The boy came up behind Bridget and jumped, landing on her back. His arm closed around her throat. He was stronger than he looked too.

"Gertie! Burn the book!" Bridget managed to hoarsely shout.

Gertie looked at the book in her hands, and the torch on the ground. She dropped the book in the fire, and it was set alight.

The boy screamed and burst into flames. He was gone.

Bridget panted, leaning against the wall in exhaustion.

Gertie groaned and kneeled. Ziggy whined in fear and snuggled up against her cheek. The ice cold of his ghostly touch brought her more to her senses as Bridget ran to her side.

"Let's get out of here." Bridget pulled Gertie's arm around her shoulders and lifted.

Ziggy led the girls out of the maze of books. Bridget carried another torch, but they didn't encounter any more of the creatures.

The librarian greeted them at the platform, a bunch of the little pathfinder lights surrounding her.

"Oh, I was just about to look for you," the librarian said.

Bridget looked at her in disbelief. How could she be so calm?

The girls explained what happened as the platform ascended with all four of them on it.

"That sounds like cursed books," the librarian frowned. "I'll send some of our ghost workers down here to search for more. I can't imagine why we'd have any in unrestricted sections."

"Maybe they missed being read," Gertie mumbled almost incoherently, leaning against her sister's shoulder.

"Is she going to be okay?" Bridget asked.

The librarian nodded. "A good night's sleep is all she needs. Cursed books take a very long time to permanently affect someone. If you would like a book on quick remedies-"

"No thanks," Bridget said quickly, not wanting to see another book for some time.

It was a long walk back to Gertie's dorm. Bridget texted Ernest, and he arrived with a rug that would float as long as he played a tune on his piccolo. It made for an interesting little parade, as Gertie lay on the floating rug, with Ernest playing and Bridget and Ziggy (who no one could see, of course) following behind.

Bridget and Ernest got Gertie up the stairs and into her bed.

"Calculus tomorrow?" Bridget confirmed with Ernest as

he left.

"Eh." He shrugged. "It looks like you have your hands full. I'll just stop by here if I find a tough problem."

Bridget nodded, smiling her relieved thanks. She set Gertie's electric kettle to boil and spooned her favorite tea into a bag.

Gertie sat up with a jolt, took in where she was and her sister standing before her, and groaned.

"What?" Bridget asked, concerned.

"I never got the Flowers of Dark Meadow books," Gertie said.

Bridget glared down at her. "Borrow them online."

Gertie and Bridget sneak out

Gertie watched as the clock on her bureau flipped to ten p.m. She heard the gentle click of the building locking up - a noise the other students wouldn't have even noticed if they weren't waiting for it - and slipped a black bowler hat on her head. She stepped in front of her full length mirror, smiled at her reflection for a moment, and reached up to twist the wing of the bumble bee brooch pinned to the dome.

Her image in the mirror vanished.

Gertie turned back and forth, as if admiring a new outfit, to ensure that all of her was hidden by the invisibility spell the hat provided. Satisfied that it was, and that she had enough magic stored away in the many accessories on her keychain if the hat ran out of power, Gertie slipped out of her room.

She had double checked during a bathroom break, and the camera in the hall still pointed away from her door.

Gertie was sure that the hat would keep her from

showing up on the camera's recording. She had acquired the hat after her mother, Eloise Mallon, was done testing a new enchantment for a camera - one that could see everything that shouldn't be seen by the naked eye. Eloise had finally created the perfect potion to spread over the camera lens to see through the hat's enchantment, but every other camera in existence would still be blind. Once Eloise knew that her brand new security contracting company had the camera that could beat any intruder, and that she could station such cameras around her house to catch sight of whatever Gertie tried to pull, she was willing to give her daughter the hat for her collection.

But even with the invisibility spell, the door to her room still moved when she opened it, which would show up on film. Thankfully, the camera was never pointing in her direction, so all was well.

Gertie slipped the door to her dorm room closed, automatically feeling for her keys in her pocket despite already knowing they were there. Her door clicked shut, locking automatically behind her.

She walked down the hall, past the bathroom, and made it around the corner to the stairwell. This door was locked from the inside, but the hallway camera couldn't see it.

My mother would make them add another camera, Gertie thought, pulling out her lockpicks.

As a security consultant, Eloise had consistently made the

point that no matter how strong a system was, someone could always break it given enough time. Once, to prove a point to a superior, she had taught a young Gertie how to pick locks. She had brought her child to a room full of executives including her manager, interrupting the meeting in progress, and placed a charmed, ten pin padlock in front of Gertie.

It had taken Gertie a while to get through it, even with the magicked picks her mother had given her to keep the lock's alarm spell from activating. When she unlocked the padlock and its shackle clicked open, Eloise clicked the stopwatch and looked at the time. Gertie nearly burst with pride at the accomplishment, but when she looked up, she saw the executives staring at her with a mix of shock and anger.

"So, as you can see, with your current plan for the Atlacorp project, my five year old daughter could break in before the guards had finished their rounds and be able to see her."

Eloise had been cited for insubordination. She quit to start her own company.

Gertie had eventually passed the lockpicking skill on to Bridget, and as children the two would help their mother test locks for her jobs.

Gertie had brought her magicked lockpicks just in case, but the dorm door was just as unenchanted as it normally was.

Idiots, she thought to herself.

Gertie heard a last click and the tension wrench went loose. She pulled down on it to unlock the door, slipped out and padded down the stairs.

The front door to the dorm had an alarm that would have to be disabled before Gertie could pick her way out of the building. The alarm would be far more difficult to get past if Gertie hadn't witnessed a teacher deactivating it with a keypad one night when he had been called in to break up an argument. The following afternoon, Gertie had experimented with turning it on and turning it back off. She assumed if it had logs that were paid attention to, someone would come around asking why she had done so, in full view of the camera. No one ever had, and the PIN had never changed. Her mother would be so appalled.

Gertie typed in the passcode and watched in relief as the blinking light changed from red to green.

The front door's lock was no more complicated than the lock upstairs, but there was a camera pointing straight at it. Gertie was unconcerned - she was invisible to the camera, so even if someone noticed something they wouldn't be able to prove it was her. There was no evidence of which room she had come from or which floor.

Gertie made quick work of the door's lock and went out into the cold air.

And collided with Bridget, who was also invisible.

"Ow!" the two girls hissed.

"How'd you get here so fast?" Gertie whispered, looking around for anyone patrolling the school. The girls headed for the front gate as they talked.

"All my roommates were in the showers so I didn't have to wait as long as normal," Bridget replied. She, too, wore a hat Eloise had been experimenting with. This one was a beanie, and had the added benefit of muffling any sound she made except speech. Gertie had permanently "lent" it to her a long time ago, once their mother had finished building a sound sensor strong enough to detect the muted sounds and given it to Gertie. "Also I made *really* good time on the floor lock. I should have checked my watch; it was probably a record."

"Nice," Gertie said.

They reached the front gate. *This* was magically charmed.

The headmistress of Flories boarding school, Abigail Clearwater, was one of the most rule-dedicated teachers the Mallon sisters had encountered at any of their schools. In some ways, this was a very good thing for the girls. While most of the non-magical teachers looked the other way when non-magical students bullied those with extra abilities, the headmistress had a zero tolerance policy. If Headmistress Clearwater found out about the harassing, slurs or fighting, everyone would be punished. Including said teachers who looked the other way.

She also insisted on keeping with the school's founding principles, that anyone who wanted to study magic at Flories Boarding School would be allowed to. If even one student wanted to take a magical elective class, that class would be held. Sure, teachers that taught magical history or potions also had to teach curriculum classes like world history or chemistry, but at least they were able to teach some magic.

Though in some ways, her dedication to rules -- like a ten p.m. curfew and magic for security reasons -- was a bad thing.

However, this wasn't the sisters' first time sneaking out. They had their methods down to a science by now.

Bridget glanced over the spell with her magical eye, able to discern, after years of practice, how it had been enchanted in the first place.

"Try a dragonfruit match," Bridget said.

Gertie pulled one of the packets of matches from her pocket and ripped off a striped match. Each of them was infused with potions and enchantments that were activated when lit. Gertie struck the flame and dropped it onto the top of one of the railings of the gate.

Nothing appeared to change to Gertie's eye, but Bridget saw the spell flicker out of existence.

"We're good," Bridget whispered, since while she could see the spell deactivating, Gertie's healthy eyes couldn't. She started climbing over the stone wall next to the gate. "I'm heading over. Don't run into me again."

Gertie followed, albeit more clumsily and with more panting afterwards, and the sisters made their way down the empty city street to the subway station.

Once safely underground, Gertie reached up to deactivate her hat's spell and Bridget pulled her beanie off altogether.

Gertie looked down at her watch as the train approached.

"Fourteen minutes! A new record!"

They hugged as the few additional passengers looked on in confusion at the sisters who had appeared from thin air.

It was a long ride, but the subway car was mostly empty so the girls murmured to each other on the way, passing time with jokes and stories.

"Mom would be proud of our skills," Gertie said, and Bridget fell silent. They hadn't seen their mother in two and a half months. She had warned them this would be a tricky assignment, and a far enough plane ride that she wouldn't be able to come home during the entire contract. But it still wasn't easy.

"She'll be done in, like, two weeks," Gertie said, rubbing her sister's shoulder. "We'll go home for the weekend. It'll be great!"

"Yeah," Bridget murmured, pulling her hair over her ruined left eye.

Gertie sighed, hating to see her sister dwelling on painful

memories.

"I spy something...green," she said challengingly.

"It is the moldy sandwich under that seat?" Bridget asked, smiling slightly.

Gertie let her head fall back onto the subway wall in exasperation. "Yes. Your turn."

"I spy something blue."

"Can I see it?"

Bridget giggled. "Nope."

It was past eleven when the girls disembarked. There were many people on the platform, waiting to board the train. All looked cheerful, and smiled at the girls as they let them pass.

"Coming from Baxter's?" Gertie asked, and a bunch nodded.

Some were holding canes or wands, others wore tall pointy hats. Bridget could see third eyes or scales hidden under enchantments and low hats and long sleeves.

There was a spark of energy in the air, as there always was when the girls finally found themselves among other members of the magical community.

They climbed the stairs into the open air and found themselves in a long line of people.

"And this is the earliest we've ever arrived!" Gertie said, staring at her watch in frustration.

"Oh, come on," Bridget said with a smile. "It's always worth it."

It took nearly half an hour, but finally they rounded the block corner and could see the green neon sign.

Baxter's Half Moon Ice Cream

The OPEN sign glowed, as it did roughly twice a month. By the time they stepped into the diner, it was almost midnight.

"Mallons!" Daisy, the hostess with flowers weaved through her hair, reached down to hug the girls. "So good to see you again!" She stood and planted her hands on her hips. "And what are you doing here? It's a school night and you could get in trouble!"

"We did all our homework," Bridget said.

"And we promise to drink plenty of black tea tomorrow morning so we don't fall asleep in class," Gertie finished.

Daisy sighed. "Like I could say no to you. Booth or counter?"

Ideally the girls would choose the counter, but that would lead to longer conversations with Baxter and Iris and any magic practitioners sitting next to them. They couldn't afford that much time when they had to head back to school soon, so in stereo they piped, "Booth!"

Once seated close to the door, where Daisy could chat with them, the hostess winked. "I'll tell Iris to send out whatever Baxter's got for you."

A minute later, Iris, one of the waitresses, brought out a large sundae bowl with chocolate and coffee ice cream, topped with fudge and whipped cream to place in front of Gertie. A large milkshake and a tumbler with the excess was for Bridget. Just what they both loved.

"Baxter says hi, and that you need to come back when the half moon is on a weekend so he can talk to you," Iris said.

"Tell him to open his restaurant during other days of the month," Gertie retorted, her spoon full of ice cream inches from her mouth.

"Yeah, because he hasn't heard that before." Iris walked back into the kitchen, emerging soon after with ice cream sandwiches and standing in front of an empty table as Daisy led a group of four to it.

"We were hoping to order-" one of the group members started.

"No ordering, sorry," Iris said, plopping the tray down.

Another member took a big bite of one of the sandwiches. "Yeah, she's right, this is better."

"You know, if you honed your seer abilities more, you could probably open a place like this someday," Gertie told Bridget. "The whole 'know what will make customers the happiest even when they don't' thing would probably be really fulfilling for you."

"I'd have to learn how to cook first," Bridget replied.

Then they took their first bite and sip of their ice cream, and all coherent thought left them.

In unison, they let out a satisfied, "Mmmm."

The ice cream was so creamy. The chocolate's flavors were so varied and had a bit of spice to tickle Gertie's tongue. The coffee still had grounds mixed in that added crunch and pungent flavor. Bridget had a "simple" vanilla shake, but the vanilla beans that Baxter used must have had some sort of magic in them to taste as good as they did. No matter how Bridget begged, he refused to tell her his secret.

Nobody made ice cream as good as Baxter. It was why - even though he was a psychic who served his customers what they needed instead of what they asked for, and even though his shop was in a city bubbling with anti-magic sentiment, and even though it was only open twice a month - the magical and non-magical communities alike flocked here.

The first time Eloise had taken the girls to Baxter's after their dinner, because they behaved, they had wanted to go back the next night. They had been so disappointed to find out it was hardly ever open. It was the perfect way for Eloise to bribe them. *If you're good for the next week, we'll go to Baxter's when it opens.*

"We should head back soon," Bridget said as the ice cream feast came to a close.

"Why? Who's going to notice anything's wrong?" Gertie asked.

At that exact moment, Headmistress Clearwater walked into the diner and locked eyes with Gertie. Their table was too close to the hostess stand. That was a mistake.

The headmistress was dressed down, wearing jeans and a heavy jacket instead of the suit that the girls normally saw her in. She and several other teachers lived on campus. They had to stay near the students in case of any emergencies.

And now she was standing in front of them, seemingly as guilty of sneaking out as they were. Gertie and Bridget would have found the situation funny, if they hadn't been waiting for the decree of detention - or worse - that could be imminent.

Headmistress Clearwater's lips pursed as she stared down at them for an uncomfortably long moment.

"I won't reactivate the gate until I get back," she finally said, and looked away as if she hadn't even seen them, resuming conversation with a friend.

"Check please!" Gertie shouted.

Iris was already placing it on the table.

Gertie and Bridget have early mornings

Since it was a weekend, Bridget skipped her morning run around the Flories Boarding School racetrack in favor of jogging out into the surrounding city of Wespire.

The city was recovering from a late night, and besides the rumble of buses and the smell of coffee and bacon, there was little sign of life around Bridget as her sneakers hit the pavement.

She had planned her run before she left, and at the giant book pavilion she took a right and ended up in one of the smaller parks Wespire had to offer. It had several paths diverging through thick trees, and little lamps hanging from overarching branches to light the misty gray morning. Bridget liked running there because the dirt path was flat, well lit, and devoid of company except other runners in the morning. The aesthetics weren't bad, either.

Bridget was listening to one of her running playlists from

her phone, not paying attention to her surroundings until she almost ran into someone.

"Excuse me-?" the short woman called, stepping onto the path in front of Bridget.

Bridget dodged at the last moment and skidded to a stop just past her.

"Sorry!" the stranger said, moving to stand beside Bridget.

Bridget sighed, and removed her earbuds. "It's ok," Bridget said, still panting from her run. "Is something wrong?"

The woman glanced up into a tree. Bridget followed her gaze, and could barely make out a black smudge in a branch before something wet stuck to her ankle.

"What-?" Bridget lifted her pant leg to reveal a green frog, sitting comfortably above the line of her sock. Her eyes nearly popped out of her head and she bit her bottom lip in an effort not to squeal.

"It's a frog," the woman said, indifferently.

"No kidding." Bridget made a face as she picked up the frog, hoping it wouldn't pee in her hand, and placed him back on the path.

He ribbited in irritation.

"Okay." Bridget took a deep breath and looked back at the woman. "How can I help?"

"A crow stole my bagel," the woman said, pointing.

Bridget looked up at the tree again, and could see the black shape flapping around.

"It's in a plastic zip top bag, so it should be safe for a little while. I'd climb myself but..." The woman gestured to her outfit. Heeled boots, a very wind-vulnerable skirt and a branch-catchable scarf.

"Yeah, no problem," Bridget said. She walked to the base of the tree, ignoring the green frogs dotting the large roots, and jumped a bit to get a hold on the first thick branch. She pulled herself up and stood on it so she could lean on the trunk to stare at the rest of the tree, trying to formulate a plan of attack.

Bridget grasped the nub of an abandoned branch as a handhold and pressed her foot against the trunk. She pushed off and grabbed the next branch with her free hand. She kicked against the trunk with both feet and got her other arm around it. She pulled herself up and swung her leg over the branch.

"You're doing great!" the woman called up.

Bridget panted and smiled down in response.

The trunk twisted at a diagonal, and Bridget was able to run up, leap, and catch the tall branch at the end. She hung from it for a moment before scrambling on top of it.

I'm certainly getting more of an arm workout than I expected this morning, Bridget thought. She paused to look at the view. The city in the early morning was beautiful. The pastel colors of the sky reflected on buildings that stretched higher than the trees, and from this vantage point she could see the spires of the magical art museum glistening in the sun.

A few more branches, and only one or two slip ups, and she had reached the crow's perch.

The black bird examined her with beady eyes. It held a plastic bag containing a sesame bagel with cream cheese and smoked salmon in his beak. The top had been torn, but the zip top remained unopened.

"I'll make you a deal," Bridget said, knowing the bird couldn't understand. There was no magic around it that her magical eye could see. The zippers on her workout jacket had little metal bobbles at the ends to make zipping and unzipping her pockets easier. She pulled one of these free from the pull tab and held it up for the bird.

The crow eyed it. Bridget watched as it moved its laden beak forward and realized it couldn't both hang onto the sandwich and take the shiny bobble. She moved her free hand under the sandwich bag.

She heard a sigh come out of its nose holes.

The bird dropped the bag with a shriek and grabbed at the bobble. The tip of his beak scraped Bridget's fingers, and she dropped it, her other hand clasping around the bagel.

The crow took off, cawing in delight at its new prize.

Bridget looked at the bagel in her hand and realized she wouldn't be able to hold it in her hands. If only her pockets were big enough. She turned the bag over and held the bottom in her teeth, not wanting her mouth where the bird's beak had been, and climbed back down the tree.

She skipped the last branch in favor of dropping to the ground, and held out the prized bagel in triumph, trying to hide the exhausted slump of her shoulders.

"Thank you!" the woman said, grabbing out for the sandwich. As her hands grasped it the crow dove back in.

"Look out!" Bridget said, swatting her hand at the bird.

It ignored her, instead landing nimbly on the woman's shoulder.

It took a moment for Bridget to realize what was happening. "No," she began.

The woman smiled mischievously.

"No," Bridget repeated. "This is one of those 'character tests' isn't it?"

"And you passed!" The woman seemed oblivious to Bridget's frustration.

"It doesn't matter that I passed!" Bridget's voice dropped to a murmur. "They're illegal!"

"What does the government know about this?" the woman asked, placing her hand on her hip. Suddenly, another frog hopped in front of her, croaking upwards. "Hush, you! I'll deal with your lot later."

Bridget stared down at the frogs and up at the woman again. "Are they...did they fail?"

"More or less," the woman said, opening the bag and taking a bite of her bagel sandwich.

Bridget watched in horror.

The woman shrugged, swallowed, and said, "Some didn't even try."

The woman looked up at Bridget and saw her alarmed stare. "Don't worry. I won't change you into anything. You passed!" When Bridget didn't look any happier, the woman sighed. "Look, I'll give you a wish. Whatever you want."

Bridget looked down at the frogs. "Change them back, no," she looked back up at the woman. "All of them. Any of them." Bridget pressed her fingers into her temple, fighting a headache and trying to think of every possible case. "I wish that, any living thing that you've changed against their will, you change back into their preferred form."

The woman huffed through her nose. "I was going to do that eventually." She reached up her hand and snapped.

Bridget's normal eye saw a flash of light, but her magic eye saw nothing.

Suddenly, Bridget was surrounded by people. All were panicked. Some sat on the nearby park benches, others had immediately pulled out cellphones, one was throwing up, and a group were gathering in anger around the woman, shuffling Bridget off to the side.

"I was late to a doctor's appointment!" One man said. "I didn't have time to help you!"

"I actually tried! Why would you still change me?" a woman whose finger bled from a large bird bite yelled.

The crow cawed back at her.

"What did my dog do to you?" one teenager asked. Her labrador barked in agreement in what sounded close to a ribbit.

"He insulted me," the woman said, glaring down at the dog.

Talking to animals, impossibly powerful magic that Bridget's eye couldn't detect, tests of morals…

"You're a fairy," Bridget said.

The woman's eyes flicked from her mob back to Bridget. "Yes."

The crowd began shouting and booing again at this revelation.

Bridget watched the scene take place, feeling not quite a part of it, when she noticed a man who hadn't been there before. A man whom her normal eye couldn't see; a man with an invisibility spell over him. Bridget frowned, glancing over him with her magical eye. It was when she landed upon the badge at his belt that she realized that one of the fairy's victims must have called the police.

She hadn't meant to warn the fairy, but something about the way she had focused on a space where there was nothing must have tipped her off.

There was another flash of light, and the crow started

flapping in place. On his back, now the size of a doll, was the woman. She wore the same modern clothing, and seemed quite out of place riding an animal.

The invisible cop pulled out his gun.

"Freeze!" he shouted, audible even under the spell.

The fairy's crow just screeched and started to fly away.

The policeman pulled the trigger, and a net propelled out of his gun. It missed the bird by feather lengths as the fairy shrieked a spell.

The officer flashed and his invisibility spell fizzled. The fairy's victims ran up to him, but he was frozen in place.

The crow flapped into the branches, over the trees and out of sight, taking the fairy with it.

The policeman's backup arrived, but too late to catch the fairy. While they took statements, and tried to free their comrade, Bridget slipped away, not wanting to be thought of as an accomplice to the fairy.

As she headed back to school at a walk, too tired to resume her jog, a black crow landed on a railing next to her.

"I forgot something," the fairy said from its back.

Bridget fought the urge to sigh and roll her eyes, not wanting to have to hop all the way back to school. "Yes?"

The crow gestured its beak forward and Bridget held out her hand. It dropped the bobble, now with a noticeable glow.

"You used your wish to help people," the fairy said. "That was very good of you. I don't want to leave you with nothing, so whenever you know what you want to use your wish for, hold this between your thumb and third finger, and make a wish. No matter where I am, I'll grant it."

Bridget knew better than to reject a gift from a fairy. "Thank you," she said, running the bobble through her key ring so she'd always be carrying it.

"Have a great rest of your weekend!" the fairy called as her crow took off.

Bridget made it back to Flories school in under an hour and went straight to Gertie's building. Holding the fairy-powered bobble in her hand had restored the energy her excursion had cost her, and she was nearly bouncing.

Bridget knocked on her sister's door. There was a groan from the other side. After a few moments, Gertie answered, in her pajamas and her hair sticking up at odd angles. Bridget could see Ziggy, their ghost dog, still in bed, whining at her presence.

"Do you know what time it is?" Gertie asked, rubbing her eyes.

"Nine-thirty," Bridget said incredulously.

"It's a weekend."

Bridget struggled to repress a grin. "Can I come in?"

"Can't it wait?"

Bridget sighed. "I saw a fairy."

Gertie's eyes grew wide. "I'll make some tea."

Gertie turns in a project

"Interesting choice," Mr. Jerson said, blinking to keep from tearing up at the overpowering smell of orange. He doubted it was a natural smell that the student had collected for their potion. Likely, they had brewed their base serum from an artificial cleaner. "Well, Miss Hanler? Do you smell your potion?"

Sitting in the storage closet, Marissa Hanler sniffed the air hesitantly. If she had brewed her Locus potion correctly, it would have magically contained itself within the classroom it was dropped into, and she wouldn't be able to smell it despite the open door.

"No," she said.

Mr. Jerson looked behind her, to the scent detector he had placed. The light was still green, so the scent he had activated in the classroom hadn't reached it.

"Nicely done." He cleaned the dropper he had used to test her potion with water. "I'm going to check your report and if my suspicions are correct, we're going to have a conversation about using artificial ingredients."

Marissa flushed as she sat back in her seat, glaring at the desk. Most students who thought that a magic elective would be an easy A often cut corners. It was nothing Mr. Jerson hadn't seen before. He picked up his red grading pen and wrote "A-" next to "Hanler" in the "demonstration" column. The demonstration grade would be averaged with her report's grade after he graded the whole stack that night.

Mr. Jerson picked up an open glass cup with a symbol for "clean" etched into its side. He waved his hand in front of the symbol and murmured "begin" in the magical language of Laux. A blue flame appeared, confined by the cup. It cast the logical opposite of the spell in the students' potion bottles, clearing any and all smells in the classroom.

"Gertrude Mallon."

Gertie perked up as her teacher chose the potion bottle with the piece of tape that had her name in her loopy handwriting. The potion she had spent a week on sloshed inside, a honey cinnamon color, as Mr. Jerson unscrewed the lid.

"In the closet, please," he said as he raised the dropper.

Gertie hurried through the grid of desks and sat in the desk chair that had been placed in the supply closet for the potion demonstration.

Mr. Jerson stuck the dropper in the potion bottle and

sucked up a few drops. He wiped the plate he had been using to activate the potion with a cloth and dripped Gertie's potion into the center.

Gertie watched as a cloud of smoke rose from the drop and *whooshed* through the room. From her vantage point, Gertie could see the cloud stop when it hit the open door in front of her, as if the door was still there to block it. She smiled, knowing her potion had worked properly.

Immediately the classroom was filled with the smell of freshly baked cinnamon rolls. Gertie had hung around in her favorite bakeshop for hours to get enough of the honey-colored scent with her scent extractor for the serum. The bakers had looked at her like she was insane as the magical tool she had borrowed from the potions lab whirred, but the fond look of longing on her classmates' and teacher's faces made it worth it.

Of course, given that her potion was properly brewed, the scent hadn't reached the supply closet so she couldn't smell it at the moment. The light on the detector remained green.

Mr. Jerson did his best not to show how pleased he was with her choice of scent. It wouldn't do well to set the other students' jealousy on her.

"Well done," he said. He placed her bottle off to the side, scribbling an "A+" next to her name. He was sure she'd earn an A+ on the whole assignment, given her penchant for writing detailed reports. For the same reason, he knew he'd find what shop made such delectable-smelling cinnamon rolls.

"Darryl Fudin," Mr. Jerson read from the next bottle.

The anxious student wearing a letterman jacket stood up. He hadn't had a choice in what class he attended this period, what with the restrictive football practice schedules. He would be the last to turn in tests, and would quickly hide the red marks when they were passed back.

Darryl sat in the closet, his head in his hands. This would be the first time the whole class would be privy to his failure. He had been up all night after a grueling practice brewing his potion, and he still hadn't been able to smell anything.

The drop of his bright purple potion fell to the plate. A cloud of smoke spread through the room and vanished.

And there was no smell.

Gertie frowned and sniffed again. That had to be even worse than a bad smell, or a smell that left the room, right? Because it was like nothing even happened.

To her right, somebody hiccupped. She thought nothing of it.

To her left, someone hiccupped. That was unusual, it was supposed to be yawns that were contagious.

Then Gertie hiccuped. Again and again.

As all the students started to hiccup in what sounded like a band of frogs, Mr. Jerson pulled out the report Darryl had turned in with his potion.

"Bends berries?" Mr. Jerson said, letting out a shriek-like hiccup. "You can't use something magical-*hic*-for your scent!"

Darryl stood in the closet, looking horrified. But he wasn't hiccuping.

Gertie was hiccuping so hard and so much it was difficult to breathe. Marissa pulled out her inhaler, feeling the hiccuping trigger her asthma. Students were trying to get to the door, to get help. As soon as they were out of the classroom, their hiccups stopped.

As Mr. Jerson tried to grab a cure for bends berries from a cupboard, Gertie struggled to the front of the class, hiccuping the whole way. She got her hand in front of the glass cup and summoned the power she kept stored in her keychain accessories.

"Be-*hic*-gin," she whispered in Laux, and fell to the ground.

The little flame lit up, and, as quickly as it had started, the hiccuping stopped. Marissa took a deep breath from her inhaler, and Mr. Jerson quickly capped Darryl's potion so as to not have a repeat experience.

Gertie leaned back against the demonstration table, panting, incredibly grateful she hadn't decided to use what magical power she had stored to fold her laundry that morning.

Darryl came out of the closet, his face scarlet.

Mr. Jerson looked at him.

"We're going to have a nice, long talk about what just happened," he said. Then he gave a small smile. "But thank goodness you were able to brew the potion to stay in the classroom."

After a moment of thought, next to Darryl's name he wrote "B-".

Gertie and Bridget doodle in class

"And then to solve the equation, you take the derivative…"

Gertie tuned out her math teacher's blather and started doodling in the margins of her notebook. She wouldn't need derivatives to calculate the revenue of her eventual enchanting store, or its taxes, or anything significant in real life.

Although if her sister Bridget heard her talking like that she was in for a lecture. Bridget loved all things math.

A large, carnivorous-looking fish took shape over the printed lines and Gertie drew some bubbles coming from its teeth-filled mouth.

Out of nowhere, a folded note landed on her desk. She opened it to see a similar drawing of the fish she had just doodled, but looking far more lifelike.

To her surprise, it began moving on the piece of paper -

swimming, actually. And then it swam right off the page, floating in mid air and blowing bubbles. Its teeth snapped at Gertie and she gasped.

"Yes, Gertie?" Mrs. Wintesnapper paused in the middle of her lecture.

"I-" Gertie looked where the fish had been floating and saw it was gone. "I, I think I just understood derivatives properly! For the first time!"

Seeing the contemptuous stares of her class, she felt her face redden. "Sorry, though, for interrupting."

When the class had resumed, the quiet girl sitting to her right leaned over. "Sorry," she whispered.

❀ ❀ ❀

Bridget walked into the cafeteria and saw Gertie sitting at a table with an unfamiliar girl.

They were laughing.

"Hi," Bridget said, as she took a seat at the table.

Gertie tilted her head pointedly to the girl. "Bridget, this is Vivien. Vivien, this is my sister."

Bridget could see that Vivien was half a head taller than Gertie, even though they were sitting, and her legs under the table reached the opposite bench. She wore a loose hoodie and jeans, seemingly comfortable despite the chill in the air.

"Nice to meet you," Bridget said.

"Likewise." Vivien smiled.

Between the two girls was a notebook filled with detailed

drawings. One page had a still life sketch of a teenage girl excitedly talking to someone out of frame, with the date and "coffee girl at Memos" written in the lower left corner. The opposite had little doodles of flowers and birds and butterflies. Gertie flipped the page, and Bridget stared at the picture of a graceful mother holding a child who was reaching out animatedly toward the front of the page. The toddler looked like he might be ready to jump out altogether.

"Those are really good," Bridget said.

Vivien blushed. "Thanks," she said, averting her gaze. Her voice was soft and had a bit of an accent from the coast opposite of Flories Boarding School's.

"Yeah, but also...," Gertie grinned. "You've got to see this. Vivien?"

Vivien cupped her hands around a drawing of a butterfly. She whispered briefly into her hands, and as they pulled away a puff of smoke sizzled off the page from the use of power.

It wasn't the only thing.

The butterfly itself, in beautiful, sketchy grayscale, flapped into the air. It twirled for a moment, showing off.

Bridget lifted her hand to touch it, and instead it landed on her finger. She jumped in surprise and Gertie laughed a little.

"Don't worry, I reacted the same way."

The butterfly took off again, flying around Vivien's head.

"Wow," was all Bridget could say.

"Get this," Gertie said. "She's only been practicing for a few months."

"I've been interested in magic for a while," Vivien said. "But my parents didn't want me taking any classes. I just learned this from watching videos online."

Gertie waved her hands wildly in excitement. "That's exactly how I've been teaching myself how to enchant!"

"How does it work?" Bridget asked, as the butterfly landed on one of Vivien's colorful drawings of a flower.

"I summon spirit energy to fill the drawing," Vivien said. "You remember when you brought your diorama to life during the history fair?" she asked Gertie. "It's what gave me the idea."

"I mean, that was me controlling the dolls with my hat," Gertie said. "But, wow, spirit energy? I've never tried that."

"Is it safe?" Bridget asked.

"Yes," Vivien nodded. "As long as I stay away from anything that would take too much energy. Like a human."

"That sounds like a challenge," Gertie said, a mischievous twinkle in her eye.

Vivien laughed nervously. "No, I think they were serious."

❈ ❈ ❈

The scent of popcorn had infected Gertie's room by the time Vivien arrived on movie night. Bridget had been hanging around all day, and Ernest had been summoned from across the hall by the buttery smell, so the gang was all there.

"We're watching *The Arrow in the Tree* today," Gertie informed Vivien.

"Going back to the classic era of animation," Ernest added, looking up. He nearly jumped in surprise when a bird poked out from underneath Viv's curly hair.

"Who's your new friend?" Bridget asked. Vivien sat down and the little bird hopped out to the edge of her shoulder. It was hard to tell that it was just a sketch, since it was even three dimensional, but upon inspection there were only a few individual feathers, the rest having been given up on for time's sake. To Gertie and Bridget's surprise, it gave out a loud *peep*.

"This is Bobby," Vivien said.

"Hi, Bobby," Bridget said with a smile. She held out a finger in front of the blue jay and it stepped delicately on. Its head bobbed about like a real bird, its pupils dilating as it peeped again in surprise.

Ziggy, decidedly jealous at this turn of events, barked to get Bridget's attention. Gertie, who was wearing her baseball cap and thus could see and hear the ghost dog, patted him gently on the head.

Bobby peeped, and took off flying around the room, landing on Ernest's head for his perch.

"Speaking of classic Animation," Ernest mumbled under

his breath.

Bridget smiled at the pun.

"Did you just make him?" Gertie asked.

Vivien shook her head. "Last night. He slept in a nest of socks."

"Wow," Gertie said, raising her eyebrows. "It's not draining you?"

Vivien shrugged, pulling her knees to her chest. "Are we going to watch a movie or...?"

❊ ❊ ❊

A month passed and Vivien became closer to Gertie, Bridget and Ernest. The four actually became a group of friends, despite Gertie's thoughts that she and Bridget wouldn't find any at Flories Boarding School. The winter snow turned to slush, and the beginnings of flowers poked through the muddy ground. The group of four did homework together, played video games on Ernest's consoles, and cheered on Bridget during her basketball games. Sometimes, when Ernest was doing homework and Bridget was at practice, Gertie and Vivien would try new spells and potions.

One day there was a knock on the door, and Gertie answered it to find a bewildered looking Vivien, with little Bobby on her shoulder. She immediately assumed that her friend had gotten a bad grade on a test.

"What's wrong, Viv?" Gertie asked, pulling her friend inside.

Vivien took a seat on Gertie's bed, shoulders slumped and her legs limply hanging off the side. "I have to go back west this weekend," she said.

Gertie could hear a sob in Vivien's voice threatening to break through, and grabbed the tissues she kept on her desk. "Oh," Gertie said, keeping her curiosity at bay. She sat down next to Vivien, offering the tissues.

Vivien ignored them. "There's no way I can take Bobby," she said, in the same flat tone. The bird pipped from her shoulder at his name. "My parents would...kill me, if they found out about him...and everything else." Viv stifled a sob, taking a deep, shaky breath.

"Vivien, are you okay?" Gertie put her arm around her shoulders.

"I was hoping," Vivien said, holding back tears. "I thought you could watch him? He doesn't eat or drink or anything, so he won't be a bother."

"Of course he won't." Gertie said. "But, Viv," she moved to kneel in front of her friend. "What's wrong?"

Vivien didn't want to say it. If she said it out loud, it would make it too real.

"I'll see you when I get back," she said. She took Bobby from her shoulder and left him on the bed.

She all but ran from the room, and Gertie was left with the little bird that peeped in worry.

❊ ❊ ❊

One night while Vivien was away, Bobby was chirping along beside Gertie as she did her homework. She had started to get used to the bird's music, and was thinking of getting her own, a real one, after she gave Bobby back to Vivien.

Then, in the middle of a trill, the music stopped.

Gertie looked up. The lamp that Bobby had been using as a perch was empty.

She sent a text to Vivien immediately, not knowing what had happened.

I couldn't spare the energy anymore, she replied. *Sorry, I should have let you know*.

Gertie sent back. *Are you ok? Do you need anything?*

No. Came the reply. Gertie didn't know which question she was answering. But Vivien didn't text back again.

❖ ❖ ❖

It started with a rumor.

Students who lived in Parr Hall were complaining of electrical problems. With the rain and thunder, faculty hired an inspector. Frayed wires and old machinery was fixed, but then students started whispering about a tall woman in black wandering the halls. The stories got worse. The students started claiming a poltergeist was living in Parr Hall. Which was impossible, given that the entire school was warded with charms to prevent any dangerous creatures from being able to enter the school, and spiritual energy inspections were done every quarter.

Gertie and Bridget still hadn't heard from Vivien since she returned, almost a week prior, and Parr Hall was her building.

"That's it," Gertie said, holding up her phone for Bridget to read.

I'm fine, a text from Vivien read. *It was a tough weekend. I'll tell you about it later.*

"I'm going over there," Gertie said.

"I'll come too." Bridget pulled her sweater over her head, abandoning the essay she had been trying to write.

Gertie grabbed her pointed-hat-shaped cookie jar off her shelf, filled to the brim with stolen cafeteria cookies. "And we're bringing these."

Bridget raised her eyebrows but didn't try to stop her.

The girls made their way to Parr Hall, Ziggy floating behind them. He started whining as they opened the door to the building.

Gertie, wearing her baseball cap, paused on the threshold. "You think there's really a poltergeist?"

Bridget scanned the lobby in front of them. "I don't see anything," she said. She certainly would be able to, with her magic eye.

"Let's go then." Gertie strode confidently into the lobby.

They opted out of taking the elevator, after hearing about all the electrical issues, and climbed the stairs to the third floor.

The halls were strangely empty. Ziggy's whine echoed behind them, and Bridget felt a tingle in her skin.

"There's rogue magic here, all right," Bridget said. "I can feel it."

Gertie, who was less attuned to such things, could only judge by the pit of unease in her stomach. "Everyone else can feel it too," she said. "That's why they're spending all their time away from here."

Suddenly, there was a bang behind them. The sisters turned, but saw nothing.

"Do you have anything with you to catch a poltergeist? Like salt?" Gertie whispered to Bridget, who almost always carried a mom-bag of necessities. Gertie hoped that salt counted as one.

"After that assembly video about the dangers of poltergeists? You bet," Bridget said, reaching into her bag to find the shaker.

"Good."

They made their way to Vivien's room.

The lights flickered as they went, eventually going out altogether. Gertie pulled out her cellphone and turned on the flashlight, so they wouldn't trip on anything in the darkness.

On their first knock on Vivien's door, Ziggy started barking intently, the tingling on Bridget's skin sparked, and a hand clamped down on Gertie's shoulder.

"Bridget!" Gertie shouted, and her sister pulled the top off the shaker and surrounded the tall shadow behind them with the salt. The shadow stood still.

The girls all but high-fived at their success. But then the creature stepped over the circle.

"Not a poltergeist," Gertie said, gripping the cookie jar close to her chest.

"Leave her alone," the creature hissed, stepping closer toward the girls. Gertie's cellphone light flickered up and Bridget could see its face. Her face. Even with the terrifying voice, the woman's face looked kind. Old and weathered. But clearly sketched.

"Vivien!" Bridget shouted, though the creature was closer to the door. "What did you do?"

The door opened. A sickly Vivien appeared and started sliding down the frame from weakness.

The girls ran past the drawing, dodging as it tried to grasp at them.

"Viv," Gertie whispered, kneeling to put the cookie jar down and wrap her arm around Vivien's shoulders.

The drawing roared at the touch. The lights in the hall flickered back on.

"Stop!" Vivien shouted at it, and the woman cowered away from the command. In the light, the girls could see she was an old woman. Her gray hair was pinned into a bun, her hands were wrinkled and thin, and her legs were covered by the skirt of her long black dress.

"What happened?" Bridget asked.

"She's my grandmother," Vivien said, looking up at the drawing come to life. The poor girl's face looked bony, her eyes sunken, her skin pallid.

"No it's not," Gertie said. "It's a sketch of her."

Vivien started crying.

"Why did you do this?" Bridget asked, looking over at the drawing.

"I missed her so much," Vivien sobbed. "I thought if I didn't tell anyone then I could pretend she hadn't...died." She flinched.

"Viv, I'm so sorry," Gertie said.

"It's all right, V," the sketch said. She tried to slither closer to the girls. "I'm right here."

Vivien looked fondly at her grandmother, wanting to believe her. "I thought I could pretend," Vivien repeated. Her voice hitched and she looked away from the sketch. "But then I saw her at the wake. I couldn't stop thinking about how she looked there...all laid out." She blinked tears from her eyes. "I didn't want to remember her like that. I just kept drawing her as I remembered her - as I *wanted* to remember her and eventually..."

Gertie rubbed the sides of Vivien's arms, trying to comfort her.

"You have to get rid of her," Bridget said.

"No!" The drawing said, her very voice sounding haunted. "No, V, please. It's me, it's your Grandma Shew. I love you."

Vivien sobbed. "I don't want to," she said, looking up at Gertie, hoping she would disagree with her sister.

"I know," Gertie said. "But look at what she's doing to you. Your grandma wouldn't want you to do this to yourself. Not for her."

Vivien nodded and closed her eyes.

By the time the sisters looked up, the drawing of Grandma Shew was gone.

"Let's get you to the infirmary," Bridget said, moving to help the poor Vivien up.

"Wait!" Gertie pulled the top of her cookie jar open, reached inside, and pulled out a chocolate chip cookie. "This will help too."

Bridget gave her an incredulous look.

"Chocolate," Gertie said. "It's known to have healing side effects."

"Keep telling yourself that," Bridget grumbled.

Vivien ate as they walked, tears dripping from her lashes.

Both the school medical nurse and healer fussed over Vivien. She was given a stern lecture about improper uses of magic as they hooked her into an IV.

She managed to avoid them contacting her parents, but as punishment she was signed up for an online course in magic responsibility.

❊ ❊ ❊

At the next movie night, Vivien arrived with a little blue jay on her shoulder. As soon as he saw Gertie, he began to whistle a familiar tune.

"Bobby!" Gertie exclaimed.

Gertie and Bridget go out in the rain

Bridget groaned as the night wind swept rain up under her umbrella and into her face. She hopped from foot to foot, trying to stay warm.

"This was a terrible idea," she muttered to herself, since Gertie certainly wasn't listening or about to agree.

The clouds were thick, but some starlight still filtered through breaks, promising the possibility of moonlight. Gertie was out in a storm, hoping for that to come true.

Gertie, of course, was wearing a hat that made her body and clothes waterproof, so she was in a light jacket over a t-shirt, unlike Bridget's feeble attempts at keeping herself warm and dry via a sweater, rain boots, and a rain jacket. She held an umbrella gripped in her clammy fingers, which was enchanted to react to raindrops by lighting up around the spot they hit. This feature was able to be turned off, but her fingers slipped too much to do so, which meant that at the moment the umbrella was reacting like it had fireworks in its material.

"Come on," Gertie mumbled, looking from the bed of flower buds on the ground to the sky.

The sisters were out in the rain for their own reasons. Gertie was there because that morning she had used up the last of her lunas buds, and lunas buds were essential for her to finish her potions homework that was due the next day. Bridget was out risking the wrath of hypothermia, because when Gertie had announced her mission, Bridget had decided she would rather hang out with her sister than go back to her room and be confronted with her roommates' glares at her presence.

It was becoming increasingly obvious to her that this was a terrible mistake, but she was freezing and drenched already, so she might as well see it through.

"Maybe we should just head back," Gertie said, frowning forlornly as she saw her sister shivering.

"No, I'm sure it'll come out soon," Bridget said. "But if I get a cold from this I'm blaming you."

Sure enough, the cloud cover broke and the moon shone down on the school gardens. The bed of flowers that Gertie had been inspecting blossomed.

They were small and white, sparkling in the light as they gathered what energy they could from the moon.

Gertie kneeled and, using pruning shears, clipped the

buds off and stowed them safely in her pocket.

"I just want to point this out," Bridget said. "You could have picked them in the day."

"They wouldn't grow back in the day," Gertie said, pointing to the little white budlets that had already grown on the clipped stems. By morning they would be half the size of the ones in her pocket, and after a few hours of uninterrupted moonlight they'd be fully grown. Gertie wasn't about to keep anyone from using the lunas buds.

"You have enough?" Bridget asked. Gertie snipped one more bud into her hand and nodded. The two girls all but ran back through the muddy grounds of the school.

They reached the dorms and climbed the steps of Gertie's building to her room. Bridget left puddles in her wake and slipped a few times, but ultimately made it safely to her sister's floor.

"I'm borrowing one of your sweaters," Bridget said when the door was closed behind them. She hung her jacket and peeled her sweater off, then rummaged around Gertie's closet for a warm, dry replacement.

Gertie, meanwhile, placed all the buds in her school-issued Advancer.

"All good practitioners know that ingredients are finicky things," an advertisement for a particularly fancy Advancer would say. *"They require a certain potency. You can't just take normal lizard tails and pop them in a bubbling truth serum batter. They need*

to be aged. Back in the Gray Era, this meant we had to hang herbs and flowers and other ingredients along the windows of cottages, or bury them for years, to dry and age. Now, we have the Skipstep Advancer! Just pop the ingredients in the top, adjust the setting, press this button, and prest-o change-o your ingredients are as old as you need them to be! Now electric powered!"

"Do you ever wonder what would happen if you turned it on with your hand still in there?" Bridget asked, wrapping herself in Gertie's down blanket.

"They have safety measures against that," Gertie responded with an eye roll.

"Because it's happened before, right?"

"Shut up."

As the lunas buds aged, Gertie filled her electric kettle with water from the water fountain down the hall. She set it to boil, and got out the paperwork for her assignment.

The Advancer dinged at the same time that the electric kettle boiled and clicked.

Gertie pulled the buds out of the Advancer, putting most of them in a tall, blue jar that kept out any light that would damage the buds. The remaining few she put in a mug and poured the hot water over.

After a few minutes, Gertie took a sip of the lunas tea. The caffeine washed over her and she grinned.

"Perfect. Now I can finish my potions homework," she murmured.

"Tea?" Bridget exclaimed. "It was just for tea?"

Gertie gave her an incredulous look. "What did you think it was for?"

"Potions!"

"Oh." Gertie took another sip. "I can see how you would think that."

"Ugh," Bridget flopped back onto Gertie's bed.

Gertie pulled another mug down from her closet. "Want a cup?"

Gertie and Bridget get the flu

Bridget couldn't stop sneezing.

This was more of a problem for her than it was for most. When normal people got sick, they would feel achy and lethargic and need to miss school. When Bridget got sick, she had visions.

She didn't get her usual visions, like glimpses of danger that could befall her, when she was phlegmy and sneezy. Instead, she saw what was for breakfast at the mess hall, what grades she would get on assignments she'd already turned in, or that she would run out of tea bags. The most helpful vision she ever got during a cold was that she'd trip over a stair. And then she did anyway.

At Gertie's (and Bridget's roommates') insistence, Bridget was staying over in Gertie's private room, swathed in blankets and cared for by her sister.

Bridget sneezed and a vision flashed before her eye. Short homework in Literature today. She sneezed again. Her mom would call. A third sneeze. Her friend Vivien needed help in Calculus.

"Ugh!" Bridget blew her nose with a tissue from the box Gertie offered.

"I'm going to go to the healer's office and get you some Quilamine," Gertie told her.

"That stuff tastes gross," Bridget protested.

"Yeah, well, watching you turn green from the stress the visions are putting on you is worse." Gertie stood, bringing Bridget's cell phone to her. "Call me if I should pick up anything else. If something goes wrong, Ernest is just down the hall so text him."

Bridget waited for Gertie's footsteps to recede down the hall. She pulled out Gertie's laptop and put on an episode of some reality show that she could doze off to.

She sneezed again and saw the winner of the show. She closed the laptop.

A half an hour later, Bridget woke up to the beeping of Gertie's microwave and the smell of orange, broccoli, and fish stewed together. She turned and saw Gertie sitting on her desk chair with a mug of green sludge.

"Drink," Gertie said, holding out the potion.

Bridget groaned, but accepted the mug. She glanced at her sister. Gertie's eyes were wide and she bit her bottom lip, as if she wanted to say something but didn't know where to start.

"You look like you've seen a ghost. Other than Ziggy," Bridget said, trying to avoid having to sip the potion.

Their ghost dog, sitting vigilantly at the foot of Gertie's bed, barked.

"I ran into Nick in the healer's office," Gertie said.

Bridget sat up, gulped down the hot potion, and put it to the side. It tasted worse than it smelled. Somehow, even with all their magic, healers couldn't make stuff that was good for a person taste any better. But that wasn't important right now. "Are you alright?" She reached forward to touch Gertie's shoulder, subtly checking for injuries.

Gertie nodded. "He was actually…" she bit her lip hesitantly. "Polite?"

"What?" Bridget couldn't believe that. Nick Coffer, polite? He hated magic practitioners, even if they'd never done anything to him.

"Yeah. He was sniffling a lot, looking for the Quilamine too. He asked about how my day was, said he hoped you felt better, and thanked me for showing him where the potion was!"

It sounded impossible.

"Maybe he hit his head when he went home over the weekend," Bridget guessed. Her nose itched and she reached for the tissues. They were just three short sneezes this time, which meant the Quilamine was working, but the vision that flashed was confusing.

She saw Nick Coffer, in his dorm room with the blinds drawn. He was eating a long, purple leaf that he tore into strips and dipped in milk.

When Bridget came out of the vision, she blew her nose.

"Anything interesting?" Gertie asked.

"Yeah. What type of plant has big purple leaves?"

Gertie pulled her laptop over from where Bridget had stashed it. She went to a botany site from her bookmarks and did some searching.

"Did it look like this?" she asked, turning the computer around so Bridget could see.

Bridget glanced over the page on "purple lace".

"Yeah. But it was dipped in milk." Bridget typed in the search bar and froze when the results page came up. "No..."

Gertie turned the computer back around and gasped.

"Oh, no. That explains it."

Purple lace leaves and milk are the primary diet of a Puddyworm. If someone you know is eating this, please contact the authorities immediately, as they have most likely been taken over.

"Do...do we tell anyone?" Gertie asked in a hushed tone.

"Gertie! Of course we do!" Bridget coughed and blew her nose.

"I'm just saying, he's really nice now!" Gertie shrugged. "I mean, he probably wouldn't give me another black eye."

"Ugh." Bridget got out of bed, putting on the winter coat she had used to walk to Gertie's room despite the sunny weather. "Come on. If he's so nice, let's go talk to him and see if the Puddyworm's willing to leave peacefully."

❉ ❉ ❉

"Oh, hey Gertie. Bridget, are you feeling better?" The Puddyworm-in-Nick sniffed, wiping his nose with a tissue. What seemed like phlegm dripping down his lip was actually just an effect of the Puddyworm's presence in a human body, as Gertie and Bridget had learned after reading up on Puddyworms during their walk over.

"A little bit," Bridget said. "We have a question for you."

"Oh, well-"

"We know you're a Puddyworm," Gertie said.

Bridget put her head in her hand and sighed.

Nick's expression became one they were much more familiar with, one of rage and promising pain. "Look, I don't want to hurt you," Nick said. "But I know this body can. And it has."

Gertie winced.

"If you're going to rat me out to the police-"

"We're not going to," Bridget said. "We were... hoping... you might leave willingly?"

Nick's eyes narrowed. "Where else would I go?" The Puddyworm asked. "Do you see anyone *willing* to hand over their body?"

Gertie and Bridget shifted uncomfortably. No one was walking in the hall, but if anyone happened to hear, they could all be in trouble.

"It's just never going to be easy again." Nick huffed, talking more to himself than them. "They finally got my last host a CAT scan and figured out he was brain dead and that I was controlling him."

"Brain dead?" Gertie repeated.

Nick waved his hand dismissively. "It's the only way to get away with controlling someone for long periods of time anymore." Nick's expression softened, as did the Puddyworm's tone. "And it seems nicer. To not have to take over a living person. I barely found this Nick in time." The Puddyworm-in-Nick's body scuffed his shoe at the carpet.

"Couldn't you just...take over a mouse and leave?" Bridget asked.

The Puddyworm scoffed. "Some life that would be." Then it grumbled. "Some life this is anyway. But I don't want to die. There aren't many of us left."

"I...I have a theory," Gertie said. She held up her phone, where she'd been reading up about Puddyworms during the walk. "We can test it before letting anyone else know this ever happened, if you'd like."

❁ ❁ ❁

"You're lucky I had leftover clay," Vivien told them. She was shaping the last leg and foot of a sculpture about a foot and a half high that looked like a little human.

Bobby, the bird that she had brought to life, peeped in agreement.

When Vivien had first made him, Bobby had been an Animated drawing of a blue jay, but she had soon realized that took too much energy for her to keep up, as Animated creations drew their spirit energy from their creators. So, she took the next logical step and made a homunculus - or a bird version of one.

Vivien had brewed a very special clay with the help of Gertie and Mr. Jerson, the potions teacher. She had shaped it into a bird, added some real blue jay feathers for suggestion, and cast a spell to take the spirit of the Animated Bobby and connect it to the magical clay.

Now Bobby was his own being, and Vivien was free to try other magical pursuits.

The goal was to do the same thing with the Puddyworm.

"Okay, I'm done," Vivien said, stepping back. She was quite an artist, and the little human looked perfectly proportioned, if only the size of a large doll.

"It's rather plain," the Puddyworm-in-Nick said skeptically. "And small."

"It'll grow. It would just take too much clay to make a full sized body." Vivien explained. "And once you're inside it, it will change according to your spirit. Bobby only had a handful of feathers when I first made his body. Now look at him."

Bobby preened, his feather-covered body appearing to change colors in the sunlight from the studio's windows.

"I guess it'll work out," the Puddyworm said, rubbing the back of Nick's neck.

"So," Bridget asked, taking a sip from her travel mug of Quilamine. "We're sure this is legal, right?"

"We're sure it's not *il*legal," Gertie responded. "It's only illegal to create a new human spirit for a homunculus. We're not doing that."

"Still, Mr. Jerson and Mrs. Ragward wanted to be left out of it," Vivien said. She sat on the table next to her little sculpture.

"They're just being cautious," Gertie argued. "This has never been done before."

"You think it would have been," Vivien said.

"Except that in the Puddyworm's native country - you know, here - all magical beasts were hunted into near extinction years ago," Bridget said, sniffling and wiping her nose on her sleeve. "Especially ones that targeted humans."

The Puddyworm-in-Nick cleared its throat.

"Sorry, uh." Bridget struggled for a moment. "What should we call you? You're not Nick."

"You're going to need a name," Gertie said, sitting up excitedly. "When you have your own body. What do you think?"

"I...I don't know," the Puddyworm-in-Nick shrugged. "How do people normally choose a name?"

"Well, are you a boy or a girl or somewhere in between?"

Vivien asked. "Or neither?"

The Puddyworm frowned. "I'm not sure."

"Maybe pick one where it doesn't matter?" Bridget suggested.

"What about Madison?" The Puddyworm asked, and then blushed. "I just...I've been Madison lots of times. Boys and girls and both. I really like that name."

"Madison then," Gertie said. She held out her hand. "Nice to meet you."

Madison-in-Nick laughed, a strange sound coming from the bully's body, and held out Nick's hand to shake hers.

"Okay, enough goofing off," Vivien said, hopping off the table. The homunculus body had to age in its shape for twenty-four hours before something could be bound to it. "Let's go get what we need."

❁ ❁ ❁

Mrs. Ragward handed over a piece of paper she had been scribbling on as soon as they entered the classroom. "I had to make some modifications to your idea," she said.

Gertie took the page she had torn out of her notebook and her expression fell at the amount of scribbles and cross outs. She hadn't had Mrs. Ragward as a teacher yet, but by the look of it she would be a hard grader.

"It had good bones," the spellcasting teacher added kindly. "You just don't know...anything about inventing spells."

"Yeah, no kidding." Gertie folded the paper and put it in her pocket. She and Madison-in-Nick turned to leave.

"There's just one more thing?" Mrs. Ragward came out from around her desk to stare down at the teenagers. "If this doesn't work...there's a very strong possibility that your friend won't survive."

"The spellcaster or the spellcast-ee?" Gertie clarified, trying to make a joke.

Mrs. Ragward glared down at her and grabbed a sculpture of a tree from her desk. The base was a large crystal, the trunk was made from twisted wire, and the leaves of delicate gold.

"This is a sculpture that holds an extraordinary amount of magical power," she said. "I'm loaning it to you now, to make sure that whoever is casting this spell *does* survive. But I expect it back. Are we clear?"

"Yes, ma'am," Gertie said with a gulp, accepting the tree that the teacher placed in her hands.

"Now." Mrs. Ragward put her hands on Madison-in-Nick's shoulders. "This is a very big risk you're taking."

"It's worth it," Madison said, jutting out Nick's jaw. "If it does work, it could change the life of every surviving Puddyworm out there. If it doesn't, then what kind of life will I even live anyway?"

Mrs. Ragward patted the side of Nick's shoulder. "Good luck," she said with a smile. "If it doesn't work I'll deny this ever happened."

"And if it works?" Madison challenged.

"Then I'll write the report and the patent and list you all as co-authors."

❀ ❀ ❀

"We got some doll clothes," Vivien said, handing over a small t-shirt, jeans, socks and shoes that were dusty and flat and looked like they had been pulled out of some old box. "For afterwards. And I talked to Mr. Jerson about any potion that could help bind the two together. He suggested coating the chamber in lunas oil so Bridget let me into your room and I borrowed some of your buds and put them through his oil extractor, I hope that's ok."

"Viv, it's fine," Gertie said, putting a hand on her knee and holding out a candy bar. "Have some chocolate, take a breath."

Vivien broke off a piece of the candy bar, all but shaking with nerves. Whenever she had tried experiments before, no one was being put at risk but herself.

"It's going to be alright," Madison said, although they had no evidence this was going to be the case.

Bridget nodded. "We can't even get started until tomorrow," she said, her voice thick with phlegm. She blew her nose with a tissue.

Some other students walked by in the lunchroom, and stopped cold when they saw Nick Coffer sitting with the freaky magic kids.

"If there's one good outcome from all of this, it's that everyone must be so confused at seeing Nick with us," Bridget said, waving at the students.

"He'll tell them, when I'm gone," Madison said.

Bridget shrugged.

Vivien wasn't listening, staring out into the distance and imagining all the ways this could go wrong.

"Come on." Gertie stood up and pulled Vivien's arm with her. "I'm starving, and you need to eat something."

"Can we go into the city?" Madison asked. "I love going to Spacer Park and watching all the street performers."

"Sounds like a great night," Gertie said.

Nobody said it, but everyone was thinking that it might be Madison's last.

❀ ❀ ❀

The group of four stood in the art studio, the homunculus body standing before them. Vivien had hollowed out a space in its chest, and brushed on the oil. It was ready and waiting for Madison.

"All right." Nick's body took a deep breath. "Do I come out now?"

Gertie nodded. She held her hand out, and the Puddyworm oozed out of Nick's nose. It was about the size of a small banana and the color of pond scum with some gray splotches. Its body was exceptionally squishy, covered in sludge that looked like mucus. It had tendrils poking out from its back that would normally be used to magically connect to and control the host, which it now sucked back into its body.

The girls only had a few moments. Puddyworms needed hosts because, left out in the open, they would soon dry out, crack, and die. They were incredibly vulnerable. The Puddyworm couldn't talk of its own accord, or eat, or even move very quickly. It couldn't smell or hear or even taste; it could only feel a pull toward nearby life. This normally helped it find its next host, so that it could take it over for survival.

Instead, Gertie shoved it into the cavity in the clay body. Viv covered it over with the clay she had dug out, and put one of her hands on the body's shoulder. Her other hand clutched the tree, trying not to shake.

Vivien took one last look at the spell Gertie had given her and inhaled deeply.

Speaking in a magical language and drawing from Mrs. Ragward's tree for extra power, she cast the spell that would bind the homunculus and Madison together.

There was a flash of light, and Vivien collapsed. Gertie caught her and reached up to stop the tree from toppling over.

"I-I'm okay," Vivien said, letting Gertie help her onto one of the art studio's stools.

They all held their breaths, staring at the homunculus,

hoping for a sign of life.

And it opened its eyes. They were a dark, earthy brown with flecks of honey. Vivien couldn't have designed the color if she had tried.

"Interesting," Madison said, their voice smooth, a bit higher pitched than Nick's had been. "It works just like a human's body. But it doesn't have any of the host's thoughts."

"That's because there is no host, there's just you," Gertie said, and held up the doll clothes. "Now put these on."

Madison continued to be fascinated with their own movements as they dressed.

Standing to the side, all but forgotten, Nick slowly blinked, as if waking up from a horrible nightmare that he wasn't sure he was free of yet. The last thing he remembered doing was hugging his grandfather goodbye, after being told the fall had left him brain dead, and then...

Nick was seized with panic as he looked around. It hadn't been a nightmare. He had been watching the whole time, unable to control himself. Wanting to beg the doctors for help. Wanting to tell the teachers that he wasn't well. Even when he had seen Gertie in the healer's office he wanted to shout and scream at her that he would never be there of his own accord.

He glared at Gertie and Bridget and they realized he was in control of his body again.

"Y...You..." He couldn't get the words out. He hated

everything they stood for and everything they were doing. But they had saved him?

"Just go, Coffer," Gertie said, taking pity on him. "You can pretend none of this ever happened, and that you don't owe us your life."

Nick nodded, the only respectful sign he had ever given them of his own free will. Then he turned and bolted.

"So," Bridget said, addressing Madison, "What now?"

"Well." The Puddyworm-in-the-homunculus sat on the table and swung their legs absentmindedly. "I was thinking I would try to learn how to make that clay. And make a whole lot of homunculi. And then maybe all of us Puddyworms can come out of hiding and live actual lives."

"That sounds-" Suddenly, Gertie sneezed four times. Bridget held out her mug of Quilamine with a smug smile.

Gertie accepted it with a groan. "Great."

Thank you for reading

TALES OF
MUNDANE MAGIC
Volume One

Keep going for the bonus story
Gertie and Bridget meet Ziggy

First of all, while I have you here, I would like to thank you for ordering a copy of *Tales of Mundane Magic: Volume One*. It means a lot to me to have readers, such as yourself, who are willing to take time out of their day and money out of their wallets to support an independent author. I sincerely hope you're enjoying the stories.

To further thank you, I have included this story, "Gertie and Bridget meet Ziggy," in this book. "Gertie and Bridget meet Ziggy" is exclusive to this published edition of *Tales of Mundane Magic*; you will not be able to find this story online.

This story is different from the others you have been reading. While the last ten stories have taken place during Gertie and Bridget's first year (their junior and sophomore years respectively) at Flories Boarding School, this story takes place when they were younger. Thus, the events in the other stories have not actually happened yet.

Again, thank you for buying and reading this book. It means the world to me.

Enjoy!

Gertie and Bridget meet Ziggy

Gertie and Bridget weren't allowed to have a pet.

It was an understanding that their parents had instilled in them. Pets were messy and smelly and took a lot of care. Care that their away-on-assignment mother and worked-full-time father could not give when they were busy enough with two preteen daughters.

But every time the girls saw a cat yawning on a windowsill, or a dog being walked, or even a hamster rolling in an exercise ball, all they wanted was to play and care for it.

This time was no different.

A small, fluffy, white and gray dog was roaming the sidewalk outside their home, stopping to sniff at plants and posts. He wore a collar, but there was no leash attached and no owner in sight.

"He must belong to a neighbor," Gertie said.

Bridget nodded.

"Hey there, puppy!" Bridget called. The dog lifted his

head, his ears perking up at the sound. "Want to play with us?"

Gertie held up the ball that they had been tossing back and forth and threw it near the dog. He raced for it, jumped into the air, and caught it in his mouth.

The dog trotted towards them and dropped the slobbery ball at Gertie's feet.

"Hi." Gertie held her hand out for the dog to sniff. He took one whiff and licked her hand. Gertie reached forward and rubbed his head.

The dog immediately flipped onto his back, begging for belly rubs.

"What a good dog!" Bridget said, petting his chest. "His owner must miss him."

Gertie checked the tag on his collar. It was too worn to read all the way.

"Is that…" Gertie squinted. "Zig?"

"It might be short for 'Ziggy'?" Bridget suggested. The dog wagged his tail, his tongue hanging out of his mouth as he waited to be pet again.

"Sure," Gertie said, answering Bridget. "Ziggy."

There was the beginning of a phone number under the name, but it cut off after the area code. Their area code.

"Well," Gertie said, flipping her hair over her shoulder. "He probably escaped from someone's yard. Let's go try to find his owner."

Bridget scooped up Ziggy in her arms, cradling him like a baby. He snuggled his head into her shoulder, panting and smiling up at her.

"He's adorable," Bridget said.

"I wish we could keep him." Gertie sighed. "Maybe, if we don't find his owner...?"

"Maybe," Bridget agreed.

They took the dog from house to house. Not only did he not belong to anyone, no one even recognized him.

"This is hopeless," Bridget said, lying on her back in their lawn as the sun started to set. Ziggy lay down next to her head, yawning from his long day.

"Kids!" Theodore, their father, yelled, opening the front door. "Dinn- what is that?"

"It's a dog, dad," Gertie said, sitting up. Ziggy ran right up to Theodore, sniffed his shoes, and yipped up at him with a smile.

"Where did you get a dog?" he asked sternly.

"We found him," Bridget said. "We spent the whole afternoon asking the neighbors if he was theirs."

"We couldn't find his owner anywhere," Gertie finished. "Can he just stay with us for one night? We'll try again tomorrow."

Theodore sighed. The dog stood up on his hind legs, planted his paws on Theodore's knee, and whined.

The girls grinned as their dad leaned over and scratched

behind Ziggy's ear, smiling despite himself.

"One night," he said. Ziggy yipped in joy as if he understood, running back to the girls and licking their faces as they cheered.

❀ ❀ ❀

"Dad's gonna yell at us," Bridget whispered as Gertie opened the door to their mom's study. The lights were off, as Eloise was out of town on an assignment, and no one was allowed in. There was too much danger from what the room contained.

The windows were covered by thick curtains; the only light they could see by were some potions and crystals that were glowing with magic.

Gertie flicked on the light switch.

"Which one is it?" Gertie asked, scanning over the many potion bottles Eloise kept on shelves.

Bridget's left eye had been enchanted in an accident, and since then it couldn't see any normal things. But it could see things that normal eyes shouldn't. Like magic.

"I only saw it once," Bridget hissed. One time, Gertie had been out with a friend past curfew and hadn't told their parents, so Eloise had used a locating potion to find her. Locating potions took a long time to brew, time one normally couldn't spend when such a potion was necessary, so Eloise always had a few stored in her study.

They'd timed their intrusion while Theodore was cooking

breakfast so he wouldn't be able to hear what they were up to. Ziggy sat attentively behind him, hoping he would drop something. Despite himself, Theodore fed the dog a couple of pieces of bacon, grinning at how Ziggy gobbled them up and immediately begged for more.

"That one!" Bridget pointed at a tall shelf in the corner.

Gertie dragged her mother's desk chair over and Bridget, the slightly taller of the two despite being younger, stood on it and her tiptoes to get one of the tiny vials of potion. A small patch of enchanted paper was tied to it by a piece of twine.

"We just pour it on," Bridget said, taking the vial, uncorking it, and pouring it over Ziggy's collar.

She pulled the piece of paper free of the twine and unfolded it. A map appeared, revealing the location of the owner of the collar and, by extension, Ziggy.

"Eastborough Mall," Bridget read from the map. "His owner must be shopping. We can bike there!"

Gertie nodded, an overwhelming feeling of sadness coming over her. But it was best that Ziggy go back to his rightful owner.

They told their dad they were going to go try to find Ziggy's owner again. He frowned, but didn't stop them.

With Ziggy in the basket of Bridget's bike, enjoying the sensation of the wind blowing his ears back, the girls rushed to the nearby mall.

"How are we going to find his owner in all of this?"

Bridget asked as they pulled up to the bike rack outside the mall. Crowds of people entered and exited the mall.

"He can smell them!" Gertie said, taking the rope she had brought along and tying it to Ziggy's collar in lieu of a leash. "C'mon boy! Find your owner!"

Ziggy barked and started pulling them through the mall.

The first stop they made was at a food stand. He sat patiently in front of the cash register, waiting for the girls to buy him a hot dog.

"I don't think that's good for you," Gertie said. Ziggy lowered his ears and whined.

"Come on, Ziggy," Bridget pulled at the leash. "We need to find your owner before they leave!"

Ziggy started sniffing again. He stopped by various potted plants and large columns that kept the mall standing.

"You think he'd *want* to find them again," Gertie grumbled, as they sat outside with their bikes again, after Ziggy had decided to pee on a fountain and got security to kick them out.

Out of the corner of her eye, Bridget saw something that filled her with hope.

"Gertie!" she shouted, pointing.

Part of the parking lot was blocked off with cones. In the center, there was a gate put up, enclosing a bunch of dogs. A sign read "Zig-Zag Dog Adoption: Come find the newest addition to your family!"

The girls walked up to one of the organizers, who wore a bright orange T-shirt with "Zig-Zag" on the front.

"Is this one of your dogs?" Gertie asked, holding Ziggy up. He barked hello to the volunteer and licked Gertie's cheek.

"There he is!" the organizer said, reaching down to scratch his chin. "We hoped someone would find him and bring him back. Or at least," she smiled, "Come and get the proper paperwork to adopt him."

Gertie looked over at Bridget, her hands full holding Ziggy. Bridget pulled out her phone and called their dad.

Theodore would never admit it, but hadn't felt relief as powerful as when the girls called and asked them if they could keep Ziggy. Screw not having enough time; they'd figure it out.

He drove over with his ID and checkbook. There was a small adoption fee, and paperwork to fill out, but the look on his girls' faces made it worth it.

Ziggy's little wagging tail didn't hurt either.

As the organizer handed over Ziggy's paperwork, and an official "Zig-Zag" leash, she grinned down at the girls. "I'm sure he's going to be with you for a long time."

Ziggy yipped in agreement.

Acknowledgments

It bears repeating that I couldn't have done this without my parents' support for my creativity and pursuit of film, acting, and writing.

My beloved sister Devyn has both inspired my writing and taught me about the craft through her insights and her own skill as a playwright.

My friends Deanna, Britt, Aaron, Patrick, Emily, Pyrrha, James, Meghna, Alex, Sahar, Ava, and Cheyenne have read early copies of stories, edited, brainstormed, and listened to me ramble on about Mermaid architecture and other fantasy topics. I couldn't have done this without them.

My extended family, Grandpas Jim and Manny; Grandmas Sandy, Pat, and Lee; Aunts Donna, Patty, Madhavi, Joclyn, and Ruth; Uncles Jeremy, Matthew, Brian, Jim, Glenn, Art, Charles, and Michael; and Cousins Cara, Joey, Joseph, Jacob and Leah, who have all encouraged my creativity for as long as I can remember, whether it be for music, improv, or through their own art. I love them all very much.

Finally, thank you to the teachers who awed and inspired me during my time in school, without whom the books I tried to write would not exist, and therefore the stories I am writing would not exist: Mr. Shay, Mr. Leal, Mr. Brunkhorst, Mrs. Chufo, Mr. Schwartz, Joey Landwehr, Professor Fox and Professor Culler.

I would also like to thank all of musical theater, because without its music, writing, acting, and the lessons it has taught me, there is no way I would have the inspiration to write.

About the author

Shaina Krevat is a software engineer at YouTube, living the dream of working for the company she used to upload to when she thought she was going to be a film director/ YouTube Creator. She graduated from UC Berkeley with a Bachelor of *Arts* degree in Computer Science, which she views as a perfect metaphor for the combination of art and programming in her life. She has spent her time creating fiction (mostly fantasy) in the form of short films, books, musicals, songs, and most recently short stories, like the ones found in this book and on her website, talesofmundanemagic.com.

She lives in Los Angeles with her wonderful dog Atlas, who constantly reminds her that real, live dogs are better than fictional ghost dogs, except when they pee on couches.

You can follow her at @shainakrevat or her Tales of Mundane Magic Facebook page.

18387485R00068

Made in the USA
Lexington, KY
28 November 2018